BLOOD TIES

A. B. PARR

Blood Ties: An Ada Picou Adventure

Written by A.B.Parr

Copyright © A. B. Parr 2022

This book is dedicated to Shannon.

CHAPTER ONE

Ｈigh in the sky, a white-hot sun, beat down upon the verdant valley. No strips or smears of white marred the blue expanse. Dry heat was part of the range and baked itself into the black soil, the gray rocks, and the horns of the cattle. Heat wrapped itself around a body and made itself known.

Sitting upon a red roan and flanked by few miles of grass, Ada Picou watched over her herd as a mother would her children.

"Where Ah come from," she muttered, "all these animals woulda drown or their hooves woulda rot off." She sat low in the saddle with her hat tilted back and she rested her hands on the horn as her eyes roamed steady and watchful. The ridges in the distance danced in the heat. Thick leather crunched under her weight while sweat pooled at the nape of her neck. She flicked thoughtlessly at a horsefly.

Despite the rewards, the challenges of cattle often irked her. Riding herd, foaling, branding, keeping the hungry wolves at bay. Ada had to admit that it was easier here in the dry hills of New Mexico, though. Raising cattle in a swamp was a nightmare.

She missed Louisiana, but not the farm where water crept up through the ground into the cattle's hooves and would cause rot. Cattle were constantly getting themselves mired and would find themselves stuck and bawling for aid. There was too much rain to work in. Everything happened in fits and starts. Water seeped into everything they owned. It dripped into the house, it came up from the floorboards, and it soaked any hay her Pa forgot to store in the loft.

Ada recalled, her Pa's dark and wet saddle drying by the fire. In her youth she would wait by the hot stove, eager with the oil. Rubbing in the oil was one of her favorite chores. She worked every inch of the leather softening it and filling the house with the smell of warm oil.

"Betterin chasin off coons and opossum," she said to herself while reminiscing.

They lost calves when the rivers came up, and occasionally there were alligators. Mostly they stayed in the water, but sometimes they waddled up and ripped a cow from the herd. It was a terrifying sight. The cow would scream and bray, eyes white with terror, and with froth flying as the alligator would flip and turn in the act of snapping its prey's tendons and bones.

Ada cottoned more to wolves. "Definitely, wolves over gators," she mumbled as she spotted a large gray wolf that loped by the eastern flank of cattle. A few others followed the leader. "This pack was gettin darin," she said under her breath.

Ada slowly squeezed off a shot and dropped one wolf, the others scattered. It was not the leader, but still a threat. While she rode herd, Ada thought of the skin and what she would make.

Coming up to it, she found the small wolf too skinny for much and decided upon a satchel. The cattle were nervous and restless. "Alright," she sighed, "Ah'll git it outta here." Even a dead wolf kept the cattle jittery. None of the herd settled until she had tied it to the roan's haunches and had started packing it back to her building.

 "Got a wolf skin here," Ada hollered for William as she carried the carcass over her should around to the back of the small shelter.

William was preparing a foundation for what would one day hopefully be a smokehouse. He whistled and smiled. "Good shot," he said as he tilted his hat back and sat on his heels. "I'll clean it," he offered.

"Nah, Ah got it, go ride the line fer a bit." Ada tossed her head back over her shoulder, indicating to the cattle.

"Alright then, I'll leave you to it." He adjusted his hat.

There was a moment of silence as she untied the carcass. They looked each other in the eye and William smiled before glancing away.

Ada frowned slightly, "ya smile too damn much William," Ada said as stabbed into the belly of her kill.

William laughed quietly before sauntering toward his horse.

Raised in Acadiana and by a French Louisiana family, Ada did not allow anything to go to waste. She skinned the wolf and before stretching out the hide over a frame. The meat was cleanly cut off and the organs separated. She salted, sacked, and buried under a stone in the floor everything that would spoil. The bones she readied to boil later. Teeth and nails would be used for arrowheads and sewing needles.

Later, William or Ada would scrape the fur from the hide and cure it. After that was done, Ada would cut it and sew it into a new satchel. She kept every item she made for as long as it would hold. She rendered fat to oil her supplies; the oil, she knew, would make her tools last longer. However, in this case the skinny wolf produced next to no lard to work with.

She gazed out over the valley as the sun set. The sky had gone from blue to purple and was edging toward gold. Ada's eyes fell upon the cattle.

The small herd steered toward a pasture with emerging green, and she could make out William calmly riding the fringes. Mostly the valley was safe without dead drops and such, but there were still dangers. The wolf from earlier in the day was a reminder to avoid getting lax. The snow had melted and the thin herd was foraging for the fresh sprouts that pushed through the damp earth.

As Ada cast her eyes over range, she realized that she was growing to feel something for this land. Perhaps, it was becoming her home, something more than a place to survive. Much of her blood was now in this soil even after the short time she had been here. She sat on her haunches and reflected upon the dead.

Haunted by a past that drove her like a demon across the country, Ada could not have peace; what she had was only the illusion. She was pulled westward by the burning hunger for revenge.

However, time upon this on tract of land had slowly eroded her rage. Now, a glimmer of a passion for ranching sprouted within her. She had followed a trail to this land; that trail had vanished and, in her search for fresh clues, came across this valley. Something about this land tugged at her. This was this land her family long dreamed of. She had the money and the grit to make it happen, if she so desired.

After eating dust for a few outfits, in addition to bounty hunting, Ada fund herself in good finances. When she was offered the deed, she purchased it. Slowly, she found herself with new goals, and this land ideally reflected these changing goals. Through the deed, she secured the water rights of a spring and a few green fields surrounded by low ridges that acted as natural boundaries and borders.

Here, Ada built a house. William helped a bit. It was just a small one-room shed with no peak, one pitch, no windows, but was built with their own hands. The house had a door on each side to let the wind through. Ada tore countless of calluses while stacking the stones, and the home they held was clean and simple. It looked more like the cottages found in the highlands of Scotland based on Ada's father's fireside stories. His unit had Scotsmen and Irishmen, and he'd learned something of their land from them.

"Children," Ada's father Joel used to say, "These folks had stone houses with thatched roofs, can you imagine?" Arden and Ada marveled at their father's words as he painted a picture of what had been described to him. "Rolling green hills, and upon them whitewashed homes the wind could never move."

"Their houses weren't raised, Pa?" Arden said.

"No, son, built of stones stacked upon one another."

"They didn't use wood?" Ada said.

Joel laughed. "No dear, stones."

Neither of the children raised in the swamp could imagine it. Even Ada still had doubts until now.

"Well, Pa, Ah kin see now what ya were talkin bout," Ada whispered as she took a long look at the solid home.

Ada had gotten the deed in the nearby town of Cerrillas. The deed was for an empty and barely used spot she could build upon. There was no timber, so Ada made due by cutting her teeth on stone.

The general store only had one saw. Mr. Carter kindly told Ada while bracing himself on his counter, "I'm sorry miss, but there is no lumber here."

The general store tilted at a gentle slant to one side, and everything was on a hook to keep it from sliding or falling. It was at enough of an angle that Mr. Carter limped when he left his shop and found himself on flat ground.

He had a sad and grandfatherly smile as he added, "Groves of trees were far and few between in this land, but one thing that we do have in abundance is rocks," he added with a wink while wiping the sweat from his brow.

Ada nodded, "much obliged, Ah know what Ah'll be needin then." She winked back.

In her younger days, Ada started with odd jobs and errands as she crossed the countryside. She made some money and banked it in the East. Later she took to bounties , and it turned out she had a natural talent for weeding folks out. Over time, her aim and her rope knots got better. When Ada slept, it was usually in a barn or under a tree. Ada stayed frugal and hungry, regardless of employment. The open road was her home and blue eyes haunted her dreams.

She had not planned on settling and was surprised by how much she found homesteading—later, ranching—rewarding. It was a marked contrast from her previous life of bloody-knuckled drunks and long rides. Growing up on a farm in the swamp had instilled within Ada an appreciation of hard work and of reaping rewards from the land.

"Work hard and good will come from it," Ada shouted when William flagged. She was tireless and she watched him drive himself to keep up. A small garden was raised quickly and a head of lean, cheap cattle started her out. However, even in New Mexico she could not shake the lessons she had learned in the swamps.

"Gotta keep the water movin." Ada glanced at the creek a worried look in her eye. She furrowed her brow and squinted. "Damn, it takes care of itself round here." Ada laughed a short dry chuckle.

William looked on in confusion. He had been born and raised in New Mexico, and Ada was practically speaking a different language. The high ground of this country was always dry. However, Ada growing up outside the Atchafalaya, had her own perspective.

"Mostly raised goats, pigs, and whatever cattle Pa could find. Water was always an issue, and it was that we had too damn much of it," she added. "Here is different; we have a crick." Ada's boots splashed through the slow and shimmering water. "Ain't no real need for draining," she realized as she frowned and scratched her head while thinking of her father. She thought back on all of the work he put into draining their little plot. "Ah kin see Pa now," Ada said as she gazed into the distance, "his hat wet, dripp'n sweat, with mosquitoes on his face and the dirt sucking at his boots as he plowed a swale." She shifted uneasily.

"What is it about your Pa and Ma," William asked. William and Ada had lived and worked together for a full season now. "You don't speak of them much," he spoke softly.

Ada's eyes rested on the western ridge. She let the question lie dead in the heat.

Cattle slowly chewed their way through the field. The night was a relief from the heat and there was a cool, damp breeze that signaled a chance of rain.

Ada's new wolf skin satchel hung on a peg by the east door. Ada and William were asleep, and Ada was gently snoring. The darkness of the desert weighed heavy like thick velvet. Outside, the small crackling fire used to hear their dinner had gone out. There was electricity in the air and the horses stamped and swished their tails. Tension wrapped around them and there was a gentle rumble from clouds that had quietly gathered above.

Faster than a heart could beat, lightning pierced the thick darkness. The eruption that followed shook the house and Ada leapt, sweaty and disoriented, from the bed. She landed on her knee with her six-shooter in her steady hand. Her yes had not yet focused and she breathed hard while poised like a viper.

She let the moment pass. Ada shook her head, rubbed her temples with her free hand, and lowered herself back into the bed and rubbed the sweat from her left eye.

William, also startled by the lightning, was stock still and watching. He lay propped up on his arm in the opposite corner of the room. He did not move; he too could feel the energy in the air.

Their beds were cowhides pulled over straw and packed with peppermint leaves. The peppermint reminded Ada of her Pa. The straw had just the right flex and smelled fresh. Peppermint she knew kept bugs out of the mattress as well.

Ada looked toward William in the dark. "Ah'd been dreaming," she started quietly as she unscrewed her flask. "Thinking back, when Ah wasn't much of nothin." Her voice barely more than a whisper, she continued, "a slick-talking preacher from New Orleans had passed through. He found himself welcomed to Ma's table." Ada coughed and cleared her throat, "Ma was wary, but Pa was caught, snared up like."

William listened as Ada sat up.

Ada's back scraped against the rough stone wall. "Pa was Southern Baptist, Joel Picou, he was called." Ada took another pull on the flask. "He enjoyed all that fire and brimstone, not believe'n much, but that man liked a damn yarn." Ada fell silent as the wind broke into the doorways and the clouds threatened their worst. "The Preacher, he talked right, he talked like he was at sermon."

William could hear the bile in Ada's words as she talked.

"Ah remember how his voice filled the room; it took up all the space to the doors, and his word, well, it was from the Bible."

William could not see Ada, but he imagined her eyes rolling at that.

"You could hear em on the porch slapping mosquitos til after midnight when the moon was straight above us." She paused and choked back something.

William sat up. "Ada…" Compassion filled the dark chasm between them.

"No, Ahmma finish. Ma, we had a fight. So Ah slept by the mules in the tack room. We fought sometimes, not terrible." Ada gave over a moment of thought to her letters and arithmetic before continuing, "Pa, Ma, Arden, and the Preacher stayed in the house. Thats where Ah found em."

Her breathing was raspy as she shifted. "Ah was up workin and gettin the day goin. Nobody else was around and the animals barely spoke up. Time got away from me." Ada rambled out. "There was so much blood... it was leakin out under the door."

William heard the rattle of the flask as Ada took another long pull.

She was no longer still. The loose gravel and dirt in the stones rained down behind her. The sound of Ada's voice moved as though she was rocking. "Ah ran. Ah fuckin ran."

Her words dissipated into silence.

William heard her biting back the flood of emotions.

"Ah ran all the way ta the damn town," she continued. "Ah stumbled in, my mouth dry that Ah couldnt talk. Ah was such a sight as the deputy was passing by that he took me ta the sheriff. After Ah said what Ah saw, they put together a posse. Tha goddamn Preacher was long gone." In a gravelly voice, she reiterated, "Ah run off. Ah couldve stayed and killt him, or at least died with my Pa."

William put his hand out into the darkness. As soon as he came in contact with Ada she swatted him away. "None a that now.

She continued quietly, "As Ah buried them, Ah looked for his eyes. He had pale and piercing blue eyes that ain't nobody got eyes like his." She paused and thought for a moment. "His eyes looked like glass or some kinda metal. He wasn't anything natural."

"Ah sold the animals, the bank took the rest," her voice fell in defeat. "Ah had distant family, but Ah didn't know em. That deputy gave me a horse from his stable, that roan outside." There was the sound of cloth rustling as Ada jerked her head toward the stables. "He told me ta try and make a fresh start." She spat and laughed darkly, "he pitied me, and it made me sick to my stomach. Ah didn't want his damn burden." Ada kicked at the opposite wall, "I told him I was gonna hunt that man down and kill him like the fuckin dog and sonofabitch that he is." Ada added a moment later, "Ah got my Pa's rifle and I hunted that piece of demon trash for years." Her breathing was heavy and the air was still. The threat of rain had passed.

William had never heard Ada say so much, ever. He dared not speak and break whatever spell was at work.

"Ah rode to New Orleans and those choked brick streets. There was nothin fer me. Some idiot built a city in a damned swamp. There was so much beauty though," she hesitated, "but Ah couldn't see it."

William tried to imagine it, but could not.

"Ah stalked the streets and the marshes, Ah listened to the folks talk, and he weren't no where about." Pain racked her voice as she continued, "Ah passed through the hills of Jackson and Charleston. Cool and shady roads took me through the Piedmont and the hazy mountains; he was ahead me of somewhere. Ah could jist feel it," she smacked her gut in the darkness, "Ah felt it here."

William heard her buckle rattle. In the darkness, William nodded, not wanting her to stop. The last of the heat lightning split the darkness and revealed Ada's red and swollen eyes. He saw her take a pull on her flask.

She continued after the rumbling died down. "In tha early days, Ah couldn't get a feel for six-shooters. Ah'd shot squirrels, sometimes rabbits, and tha occasional opossums. Ah'd been good with Pa's rifle." She shifted, "Arden tried, but he couldn't aim worth a shit. His breathing was always wrong and Pa would have taught him better if he'd had a chance."

Ada was speaking so low that William had to strain to hear her. This was the first he had heard of a brother.

"Arden wouldn't commit to the shot. He was young and it didn't come natural like it did to me." She was trying to get the words out in such a hurry that they ran together. "Huntin made sense too, the animals made sense." Ada paused. "Huntin men weren't no different."

William waited with bated breath. He was confused, but wanted to be a comfort. He heard Ada shift against the wall as she came over and laid back down on the straw, finished with the talk. Her empty flask fell to the stone floor.

William knew she would say no more.

"Morning," William greeted Ada as she limped into the light while shielding her eyes.

"Damn bright out, ain't it," she asked.

"Bone dry," pointed out William. "Didn't get rain last night."

"Nah, Ah guess not," Ada stumbled over to the bench by the fire pit they had dug out.

"Coffee is still hot."

She nodded and poured herself a heaping cup of the thick black tar.

"Made it strong for ya, last night-"

"Werent nothin," Ada growled. She drank while rubbing her eyes with her free hand.

No downpours followed the heat lightning; the morning light sparkled with dew. The cattle rolled the soft and wet grass in their maws, the embodiment of content and calm as their lowing echoed off the distant canyon walls.

Ada noticed a strange peace settle into her bones. She used to see only red. How many times, she thought, had she woken up in sweat dreaming of blood and death? She even imagined screams that she never heard.

"Ahmma get to it then," Ada had a hard time shaking off the previous night. Still unsettled, she turned to work as a form of distraction.

William nodded to her. He carried a worry in his eyes for her.

Ada walked over to the roan and brushed him down before she put his saddle on. He was stubborn and it took a bit to get the girth to lay tight. She had to walk him and let him breathe out his morning itch before he calmed down enough to ride.

Ada stepped into the saddle and rode out to the herd. It was not a large head of cattle, but the number they had was enough. The herd was manageable on the land that trapped them. Some would think this land lucky upon seeing it. However, they would be mistaken.

Ada was aware that she had not gotten lucky. Ada did not cotton to luck. She dug in for this spot. After following the Preacher past the Mississippi through fields and prairies, the trail had gone dry. She found herself in a small town on the edge of wilderness.

Ada spent a few seasons in the area getting acquainted with the place while waiting for the Preacher's trail to reappear. In that time, this raw and wild land grew on her. There was something about the region that called to her. The basin where she grew up with similar. It was wild and untamed, it was nothing something could break. A person had to see the beauty in the harsh land; when they did, they were locked in. This valley had been owned by Jack Flynn. He had not worked it and had been run off it. He lacked the experience necessary to see the beauty and live off it. Ada had learned from her family and the Natives all she needed. It was as though she were made for this land.

Back east of the Mississippi, she hunted deer with Choctaw and Chowanoac. She always tried to make connections with Native people wherever she went.

"Watch and learn," her grandfather had told her and Arden.

Ada could read a horse, the animals she hunted, and the folks she ran across. That same intuition is what kept Mary leery of the Preacher and successful at bounty hunting. Ada treated encounters with strangers and the first people like she did wolves and bears. Respectfully, she learned the ways of the tribes. She was often welcomed, although often coolly. She had helped women deliver babies and cared for pregnant mothers on occasion. She realized that these were the only families she had left.

The Tepehoan helped her find this spot. Ada had spent time with them and earned some respect. It was a land of good grass, shelter, and water. Too close—for them—to the town which they saw as a threat. The black soil was rich in fertility, yet also had dangers. Ada lived, and learned, among the Tepehoan for a season. When returning from a bison hunt they showed her the valley. Ada had dropped a bull with her Sharps 1874 and she carried medicine made from that bull in her satchel. The Telehaup had told her it was a good grazing spot.

Ada accepted the opportunity for distraction. Here, she decided, she would establish herself. The Preacher's trail had gone cold for two seasons now. It angered her to lose him, but she pondered if he may have met death another way.

The small home she'd built was stocked with meager supplies. Mostly it was occupied by tools and foodstuffs. It lacked windows, but the two doors allowed a good breeze. Opening both one could see the sunrise and sunset if they wished. Located on a gentle rise, it avoided the heavy runoff from the ridges above. After the home was built they fashioned a chute for branding on the north side of the home. Ada also added swales to each side of the shelter that sent water to a garden located on the south side. They grew kale and spinach and ate it with dried meat. They expected the cattle would get fat and produce a nice profit for the year. Ada imagined that she would do well settled here.

Sweat rolled down Ada's back as she tilled the soil that would become a garden. The plots were too small to use a horse , but the hand tool that William brought from Mr. Carter carved and rolled the soil in Ada's steady hands. The cracked earth peeled back and revealed good soil for growing. Ada toiled tirelessly until dark brought supper and night brought exhaustion. Bone tired, too tired to dream, that was her goal. Going to sleep exhausted every day did not give her time to much worry. She supped after dark. Breakfast, she enjoyed before dawn. Usually, she ate jerk for lunch.

She slept like a log when she did not have nightmares. As a bounty hunter east of the Mississippi, she found she was a poor shot with her six-shooters. Most crimes were white-collar, but not all. Ada had gone after kidnappers and murderers. These always got her worse side; if she did not beat them to death, she got close. Most bounties for kidnappers, murders, and those of a carnal nature were marked to be delivered or dead or alive, which was good enough for her.

"I heard of ya," the drunken man drawled as another snickered. "Yer Joel's kid, Picou, was it."

Ada tensed, her eyes going cold. She had only just sat at the bar and ordered a drink while looking for the bounty she was trailing.

The two men laughed. One was her bounty.

She downed the drink and stood.

"Oh watch it now," the friend said, "she's riled. Heard she was the one that brought in the twins hiding out 'round S———— ⋆ · ☆ · ⋆ ————."

The bounty took a draw on his liquor. "She ain't but a little shit, mom though, Mary was a fine woman from what I—"

He was cut short as Ada threw her knife and pinned the bounty's hand to the bar.

"Yeow!" he yelled as Ada sauntered up to him.

"Ah guess nah yer done talkin yer ridein with me." She cocked an eyebrow at the friend as he made a hasty retreat.

"God damn you woman—" the bounty started.

She clubbed him over the head and he only awoke after she'd trussed him up on her horse. "Ya behave now, or don't, yer call," Ada said as she sat low in the saddle and gave the red roan a kick.

As Ada sat watching over her cattle and recalling the past a sound in the distance made it to her ear.

Horses were crossing her land carrying riders of the Tepehuan. They were a local tribe she had broken bread with. Despite the distance, she could see a successful hunt. There were many carcasses.

Ada raised a hand and the gesture was returned. She settled into her saddle and waited out the day. It was hot, almost always hot. Aside from a few weeks in winter and wet days in spring, it was always hot.

Louisiana had been hot, too. This was just a less sticky hot. She wiped at her brow and chewed on some jerk as the roan grazed. The cattle ate peacefully and without worry.

Another horse and another rider appeared in the distance. This one was a townie. He rode in slow and deliberate. The cattle barely noticed.

William, she was fairly certain. Ada watched, the rifle across her lap not looking to take chances.

"Afternoon, Miss Picou," William said warmly as he rode up. "No work at Mr. Carter's this week for me, so here I am." He gave her smile.

Ada looked hard at him, he was a young man with a large handlebar mustache, lean, and tall. She nodded, waiting expectantly for a reason as to he was back early. His new hat, clean in the sun, almost made her smile. She refrained, knowing he would be embarrassed.

"Mr. Guilford said to come by when you can. Said, it was about your deed," William stated.

Ada prickled at both the summons and the topic. "Ah'll   be around," was her offhanded reply. Before the summons, she was thinking of offering to William that he ride with her. But now her ire was roused.

"I'll head back and work on that foundation," William offered, confusion clear in his gaze.

All she had for him just then was a nod.

At the end of the day, she returned to the fire pit. She was always thinking on the food, coffee, and warmth it offered.

Ada did offer William coffee and said, eyes focused on the distant horizon, "It ain't ya." "Jist got me thinkin bout this land is all," she added, "what it means." She gestured across the vista with an open hand. "Ah think Ah want to hold it fer a bit," she added.

They sat in silence while studying the valley. The coffee was thick and dark. She held it close to her and took in the warmth from it. The heat from the cup settled into the bones of her hands and calmed her. Her time in the south had given her an appreciation for, and skill with, chicory.

"Damn, you whip up a strong brew," William coughed.

"William was a good fella," she thought to herself as she gave him a little smile over the rim of her tin cup." "If a little green," she added.

He had a nice jaw and thick black hair that ended in curls.

"Yea," she thought as she watched him, "he's alright."

The sun was setting, and eventually the only light came from a small, hot, sputtering tallow fire. as they roasted a bit of beef on a spit.

William dripped the grease back onto the beef from the pan under and inquired about the ranch. "You want to stay," he asked.

"Ah ain't sure," she replied honestly, "Ah'm not sure what that looks like."

"It looks like this, Ada Picou, just like this," he smiled.

"Past six months've been good," she admitted. "No hitch to speak of really," she said while speaking low.

"Aside from eating snake and wolf more'n I'd like," William added. He tossed her his flask of rye.

They talked about the land longer than they intended. The moon hung high by the time William realized he had been watching her close. In a fluster, he got up and excused himself. Tomorrow would be another long day. There was always work to be done, but he liked that.

Ada got up and went to the roan's stall. "Hey boy," she patted the horse. She took out the brush and started working her way around him.

As William picked up around the pit, he pictured the care and time she always spent on the red horse. A little red jealousy crept up his neck and he chased away the thought upon realizing his jealousy of a horse. He kicked out the fire a bit harder than he intended and snuffed out the light of the coals.

After brushing down her horse and picking his hooves, Ada slumped onto the stoop.

She listened to the sounds of the night. The far-off call of a coyote, lonely and without answer, echoed. She listened to the babble of the stream and it settled her mind. She leaned against the stall, the hard and rough wood a comfort. She appreciated what the land offered, the harsh beauty of life and death.

Ada's knotted muscles unwound as the wind played across the grass. She sighed while looking at the cattle, knowing intimately the challenges her father had faced on his farm. This was her land and she belonged to it. Ada thought about her father and how much he would have loved it here as she slid down into the shade and dozed off.

Ada dreamed of her family. She saw her Ma, Pa, and Joel Picou fleeing the flames of war. When the war came, soldiers took everything not nailed down in the name of the war effort. Joel had a cousin that helped them escape across the lake on a ferry. They fled to New Orleans where they lived on in fear. Later, they carefully made their way across the Atchafalaya basin. Panthers, bobcats, and alligators kept them up at night and in constant terror. The dirt roads they took were flanked with snapping turtles, alligators, and occasionally soldiers. Mary's horse lost a leg to one of the alligators.

Stirring, Ada took a moment and thought about all that she left behind. She realized afresh that everyone she had loved was now dead. It was a sobering thought.

Ada stood and turned with her hoof pick in hand to the horse. "Ah know it ain't necessary 'round here," she talked to the horse, "but Ah like doin' it."

The red roan stood still and let her do her work. She studied the horse's feet. The hoof walls and frog stayed firm, dry, and only needed trimming and filing every few months. Ada did it regardless of need; the horse was a final tie to her home. The motions of caring for the horse gave her comfort. In the stall, she could remember what it was like; the smells did not change. She could picture her home before the Preacher. When she finished, it was dark and she was alone. The only sound near her was that of William settling in for the night.

The fresh thought of the Preacher had her on edge. Ada was still as a stone, and nearly as immovable. Her muscles were tense as though ready to spring. Nothing happened, nothing moved. She stood, stretched, and shook her head.

"Damn, Ah'm gettin jumpy," she said to no one.

Ada washed her face in the basin of cold water collected from the stream and laid herself out on her mattress. Ada shuffled past William. Looking down at him, she realized that Arden had the same dark curls. As she lay down, she considered that Arden would be William's age.

"Instead," she thought, "he's in the cold dirt." Ada's sleep was not peaceful.

CHAPTER TWO

"Ada, I'm heading to town," called William at dawn.

She looked at him and nodded.

"Going to do a bit for Mr. Carter," he continued, "I'll get us some more coffee."

"Thanks, Ah'll follow after Ah see to the stock," Ada replied. "Mr. Guilford was decent enough, for a lawyer," she thought as she cinched the roan's girth once the cattle were seen to and everything patched up. She patted the horse. "He's composed and reserved, like you boy. He don't mince no words." Ada had appreciated Mr. Guilford's no-nonsense nature from the time she first met him.

As she rode, she thought over the bounties that made her the money to purchase the land. She talked to the roan, saying, "Too many men, 'specially back east, talk too damn much. They'dd run their mouths and say nuthin." Her mind wandered to quiet William. "Like they was tryin to win a tongue waggin race," she talked softly to the horse.

The roan chuffed and shook his head.

"Paid well though, didn't they," she asked the roan as she stepped up into the saddle. Not all the bounties were wanted dead or alive. She had to exert control with quite a few of them. As a bounty hunter, she was generally professional. Her temper occasionally got the better of her, but bloody and bruised was still "alive."

One of her bounties once offered her a large sum of cash to turn a blind eye; a temptation for someone without any steady work. But

Ada's reputation would have suffered and nobody would hire her if word got around. That well would run totally dry if she had taken the bribe. It would've cost Ada her the hard-earned reputation and she did not take to that loss. That bounty found himself hogtied on the back of her horse. Ada took that particular ride back slow and only had to knock him out a few times in the ensuing days. He was ready for the cell when she dropped him off.

When she arrived, her mind was on Mr. Guilford. She cottoned to him, he did not talk much and he was a man of means. "What's there not to like," Ada patted her horse. Mr. Guilford was not an overly kind person, but was an honest one and kept a good ledger.

Rifle in its scabbard across her back and six-shooters tied down, Ada walked by the false-faced buildings. She was heading toward the lawyer's wooden sign that flapped slowly in the hot breeze.

Ada had been in and around this town for over two seasons. People had gotten used to seeing her, even if she kept her distance. Faces new and old greeted her in a friendly manner, albeit at a wide berth.

She walked with a different swagger than the townsfolk. They saw it, knew it, and avoided trouble as best they could. Ada's countenance was not sour though, she was just steady. People generally took well to her and her straightforward ways. Men tipped their hats and women would nod respectfully. William greeted her at the general store and she slipped him a list of supply needs from across the counter.

"Pretty day ain't it," William asked.

Ada shook her head. "Yea, it's somethin alright."

Mr. Carter came out of the back with small parcel. "William can you get this to Ms. Peace when you're done," he asked while handing William the box. "Her young ward asked about something to scour with." He looked over the counter to Ada, "Good afternoon Miss Picou," Mr. Carter said with a kind and genuine smile.

"Afternoon, Mr. Carter." Ada softened a bit, "Pretty day, ain't it?"

William could not suppress a smile.

"Yes, it is miss, yes it is," Mr. Carter said as he gazed out the warped and fogged glass. "Hope you're getting along alright," he added.

"Course Ah am. Ah got William out there," she looked to William with a challenge in her eyes. "He's almost done with tha smokehouse."

"Good to hear Miss Picou, I knew you'd do just fine out there on Jack's place. He really took to you." Mr. Carter sounded winded. "I need to go sit for a spell, you take care now Miss Picou." He wandered to the room behind the counter in his crooked way.

William deftly prepped Ada's purchases. "You want me to pack it up," he asked.

"Yeah, but that don't get ya outta that smokehouse none." Ada grabbed a piece of candy as she walked out the door. Back in the sun, she could think. There was something about being indoors that put her out of sorts.

As Ada stepped into the sandy street she saw a carriage pass in front of Ms. Peace's place. Golden dust, glowing from the sun, hung thick in the air.

"Ah need a good flatbed wagon," Ada said rubbing at her neck.

"Excuse me ma'am, are you talking to me," a stranger spoke up.

"Nah," she said in a distant tone. "Just makin plans." Before Ada could secure a wagon, she was to see Mr. Guilford. He was the reason she had come to town.

The sounds of boots on wood and people chatting filled the air. A sign proclaiming "Guilford Lawyer" gently swung in the heat.

Ada opened the door and stepped into the dark office. As her eyes adjusted, she saw two people sitting at Mr. Guilford's desk. The man smiled at her, not knowing her, with a large mouth full of teeth. He had uncanny piercing blue eyes.

Recognition erupted in Ada and her hands flew down to her six-shooters. Across from Mr. Guilford was the Preacher. She fired wildly into the office. Mr. Guilford dove under his desk as bullets ripped into the wood surface and sent splinters into the air.

The creature that had killed Joel, Mary, and Arden was right there.

The Preacher leapt behind an old chifforobe that Ada perforated with bullets. Ada was gnashing her teeth and had bit through her lip. The monster that cut Arden's life short was less than ten feet away.

Mr. Guilford yelled for her to stop.

Her bullets spent, the empty chamber's clicks were deafening. Ada threw both pistols down and was going for her rifle when the Preacher attacked.

He was bleeding and desperate. His first swing was wide as he jumped toward Ada, but she flinched back and he caught only air. She dropped her stance low and swung tight with a left and then a right. Both connected and the man with the blue eyes stepped back, almost tumbling over a smashed chair.

He stepped wide and came in with a determined eye and a right uppercut that took the wind from Ada. He followed with a left hook to her jaw. She dropped to her knees as her head snapped to the side. Still bleeding, the man looked her over a light in his eyes, as a commotion outside the office grew. He kicked open the door and ran through the gathering crowd to his horse.

He was gone.

She heard his voice, but no words registered. Ada moaned and was sick.

"Hold on there, Miss Picou," said Mr. Guilford. "There is nowhere you need to be right now," he added. "Thank you doctor, I think we have it here."

"We ain't got shit," Ada mumbled as she blacked out again. Someone was yelling. She was caught flatfooted. After all of those years. The yelling cut the air and made her head shake.

"It'll be alright," said William. "You're having a nightmare," he continued, "just rest." William rested a hand on Ada's and she didn't pull away. Her hand was small, cool, and hard in his.

Ada heard William retreat to another room.

"What happened here, Mr. Guilford? I don't understand," William said.

"She came in and just started shooting the place up," that voice, Ada recognized, was Ms. Peace.

"She did indeed," added Mr. Guilford. "I was talking to one of the new Diamond B. hands and well, you see what followed."

"Is she getting arrested," asked William with concern in his voice.

"Ada's ways aside boy, this is serious. She shot up my office and an employee of Mr. Minger's," answered Mr. Guilford. This town has laws and I will talk to the sheriff."

Ms. Peace shot Mr. Guilford an eye when he mentioned the man who had come from Boston. "Right now, she has to heal," added Ms. Peace. With that, she set the men away.

Visions of her parents and brother flooded Ada's mind and sweat rolled down her temples. Ada was still filled with white-hot rage that pierced her from her depths.

Someone was tending to her. Her eyelids fluttered and through her lashes she saw Therese. Never had they spoken since Ada had come to town.

The hand of Ms. Peace came into view, and Ada realized she must be at Peace's place.

Therese was saying something under her breath in Spanish. Ada recognized prayers when she heard them.

"Ah ain't dead yet," she croaked.

Therese darted away.

Ada overheard the conversations and started to puzzle them out as her head cleared.

Mr. Guilford had said the man she saw in his office was a new hand with Diamond B. A man owned it from Boston. What was happening around here?

"Bastard deserves a slow painful death," Ada said in a grating voice.

The office was pocked with bullet holes. Bits of wood had been swept up and the furniture righted.

Ada noticed dried blood in the cracks of the floorboards.

Mr. Guilford's knuckles were white as he sat with Ada and the town sheriff, Johnny Pile. Ada clenched her jaw, she had a blackened eye and a bruised jaw.

"Miss Picou, what you did here was illegal by all accounts," observed sheriff Pile while looking to Mr. Guilford for support.

"Yeah, he's a bounty a mine," she replied.

Mr. Guilford sat back in his chair, rubbed his temples, and sighed deeply. He was a big man, over six and half feet tall, and broad-shouldered. Wrinkles wrapped his eyes and his black hair was framed in gray. His suit was almost black. "You almost killed me Ada," he slammed his massive hand on the desk. Loose wood from the bullet holes bounced on the surface.

Ada hung her head and replied, "sorry 'bout that," while she struggled to maintain her calm.   "Tha man ya had in yer office is a murderer and needs to be shot dead."

"Even if you were hunting a legal bounty, which I still need to confirm, you can't shoot up Mr. Guilford's law office," sheriff Pile said while red and frustrated.

"Mr. Guilford, you were the only witness. I If you don't speak up, there is nothing that I will be able to do for you," and he added, "or this town," casting a cool eye on Ada.

Everyone could hear Ada's teeth grinding as he spoke.

"Who was that man anyway Guilford," asked Pile while settling back into the cracked chair.

"New man on Diamond B, He's working for Minger's outfit," Guilford answered.

"I hear he paid cash money for his metes and bounds," Pile was fishing, Guilford knew it when he saw it.

"I don't speculate Sheriff." Mr. Guilford stood. "I will handle this particular situation, thank you Sheriff, good day."

"Well, I just know he was after Old Jack's, so I thought—"

"That will be all Sheriff. Again I bid you good day." Mr. Guilford towered over the Sheriff and Ada.

Sheriff Pile excused himself and left.

"What's in his craw," asked Ada trying to lighten things.

"Nothing that concerns you, Miss Picou," Mr. Guilford sat himself slowly back into his chair. "I will be sore for days because of you. Do you think I fit under this desk?"

It took her a moment to register the joke before she let out a chuckle. "Ya did look a sight." She sat quietly and reflected on the previous day. "Genuinely, Ah'm sorry Ah shot up yer office," Ada spoke softly and sincerely.

"Nonetheless, I have sent a message to get that man's name from Diamond B. and am sending a wire to verify that he is indeed a wanted man who you are collecting a bounty on. I was unaware that you, Miss Picou, were a bounty hunter. There were no indications since you had arrived that we had someone of your ilk in our town." Mr. Guilford looked down upon Ada reproachfully. "That is information you should have disclosed."

Blood dripped from the cuts Ada scoured into her palms as she squeezed her fists.

The blue-eyed man Ada knew only as the Preacher rode hard and soon found himself in the Diamond B. stables. Reginald Minger also found himself in the same location.

While the new hand put his horse in a stall, Minger was sharpening an axe. A pile of headless chickens lay at his feet and his hands were covered in blood and feathers.

"What the hell happened to you," asked Reginald Minger.

The man with blue eyes leaned up against a post and took a long pull from his flask. "I had a run-in with that crazy bitch that owns Old Jack's place." He winced when he spoke.

"Go get that looked at," Minger threw a nod to the ranch house.

The blue-eyed man scowled and limped to the house while deep in thought.

"Who is this Ada Picou," Minger wondered as he slid his thumb across the honed edge of the axe.

As the sun went down, the evening saw Ada and Mr. Guilford sitting in Ms. Peace's boarding house and sharing a meal.

"Ada, I am worried about you," Mr. Guilford said as he sipped his coffee, "I saw you ride in and win over Jack Flynn and Jim Carter. What in the world came over you? I want more than what you have volunteered thus far."

The concern in Mr. Guilford's eyes softened Ada a bit. "Ah owe ya more than a shot-up office," Ada said while tearing a biscuit. She sopped up some gravy and gathered herself.

In the quiet of the evening, she told him of her family and the Preacher that had ended them.

"Well, Miss Picou that is quite a tale." His eyes were wet and hands trembling slightly as Mr. Guilford stood. "I will see sheriff Pile about that man. Miss Picou, you don't have to worry yourself with him any longer." His giant hand patted her shoulder.

The weight of his hand comforted Ada.

Ms. Peace tossed them a wave as they stepped out into the night together.

"You know of Reginald Minger," Guilford asked Ada.

"Nah, never heard of him," she drawled, "how come you ask?"

"Well, Ada, he's hungry for land. He's been searching for Jack Flynn the past few months."

Ada was surprised. "That's who sold me my land."

Mr. Guilford nodded, his face illuminated in a golden aura as he lit a cigar. "I told him the land was sold and he thought I'd bend like his cronies back east," he chuckled. "Minger's not used to folks with a bit of mettle." Guilford paused for a moment and admired the night sky. "He struck me as a surly man too used to having his way." He shifted his weight and leaned against a pot that groaned under his weight. "Now, knowing about that man with the blue eyes, I just want you to be careful."

"Ah don't know 'em, or of 'em," she stated matter-of-factly, the mention of the Preacher again getting her hackles up. She was resolute and still. Ada knew Guilford would go to Johnny, the sheriff, but in the meantime, she had a hunt to get back to.

CHAPTER THREE

Ada woke to the soft movement of hooves across the grass along with the breathing and chewing of many animals. Dim light ebbed through the cracks around the door. Her body stiff and aching, she rose slowly. After adjusting her shirt and setting her hat upon her head she made for the door, retrieving her rifle as she went. Ada pushed open the door to greet the day.

She was not alone.

Staring up at her from across the cold ashes of the pit was a dog. It was a scruffy blue heeler that panted as it watched her. He had mottled black and white fur that was matted and coarse. Nearly hidden were brown blotches lacking any dominance.

Ada turned in search of anyone who might've accompanied this animal. There was no one about, and the valley was clear of riders. Out of habit, she looked to William.

He was not there. William had not yet come back from town and was probably logging more hours for Mr. Carter.

Ada found herself alone with the newcomer.

She lowered herself into a crouch. Ada cut her eyes to the sides and held her rifle at the ready.   She verified for a second time there was no one around to shoot. It was just her and a dog.

Curiosity and confusion were mirrored in the animal's eyes. They squared off for a moment. The air was still and warm, and there was not yet a breeze.

The dog reached a leg up and scratched behind his ear. His eye never strayed from Ada.

"Bad place to git lost," she told him.

His right ear twitched.

"Ya look like ya belong with someone." She looked around again with a scope she kept in the saddle bag hung upon a nearby wall. "Ya hungry boy? Ah don't see nobody to claim ya," Ada said as she turned and pulled on her boots. The rifle she carried was momentarily set aside and propped next to her against the wall. She wrapped her belt around her waist, grabbed her hat, and turned. "Now, what are we..." she trailed off. "Gone," she proclaimed to empty air.

The blue heeler had darted off toward the western ridge of the valley.

"Git on then," she shouted, as she crossed to the stall. "Shouldn't be out here anyway," she said to the roan.

Like everything in the valley, the stall was half stone and half dirt. Aside from the doors on her home which were given to her by Jack who had previously used them as part of a wagon, this stall had the only wood. The roof over the roan was made up of a chunk of old town walkway that had ripped free in a flash flood that Ada found wedged in a gully when she first came to town.

The sweet smells of hay and horse sweat filled the air. She enjoyed a deep breath and stretched.

"We gonna have to hunt soon," she said to the roan. "It'll be man er beast. Maybe both." She brushed the red horse's mixed white hairs.

He gave a gentle knicker and leaned against her hands, enjoying the attention.

Ada brushed from his neck, on each side, past his mane. The heavy wooden brush had a good weight. It ran through his coat down from spine, to withers, back to spine and down to belly. His legs were each brushed and then the brush itself cleaned.

When she had been younger, Ada had braided horse hair, or woven it in hers. Now she let hers hang and cut it with her knife when it got too long. She still wove with the strong horse hairs, but only into tools for her use.

The brushing done, Ada picked at his hooves. She carefully ran the small rounded blade on the inside of his hoof wall. She scraped out the bits from around his frog and made sure no rocks had lodged in. She was mucking out the stall when her eyes strayed to the horizon.

The dog was standing on the ridge.

He sat still like a guardian or lookout.

Saddling her horse, Ada prepared to ride out to her cattle. She left a pot of water and some jerk by the coals. "Ah won't see no animal go hungry," she thought. She figured the only animals that needed to suffer were those that brought it upon themselves.

The men that she'd hunted came to mind. She'd crossed paths with some of the worst of their kind. "Some folk seem to need their suffering." she told the roan as she put away her hoof pick. "It carries them through life like a raft." She put the thoughts out of her head as she stepped into the saddle.

Her mind cleared and her worries fell off her has they caught a breeze while riding out to the cattle.

The small herd gathered around the spring. It was less than a hundred head, but enough to start and to satisfy her needs. She kept a close eye on the older heads. Those she might have to butcher earlier, likely too old to survive the stockyards.

Ada spent time and care on a bull or heifer she had to draw out to cull. Her shot would be clean when the time came.

"Figure, on one a year," Jack had told her.

Ada had only two mouths to feed and she was frugal. "It's alright," she told him, "Ah don't mind huntin. It's sumthin Ah'm good at," she said as she gave Jack a rare smile.

"You know anything about cattle," Jack asked.

"My Pere was a butcher and my Pa raised a small herd in Louisiana," she answered.

Jack eyed her curiously. "Louisiana, huh? I think I know of your people, the Picous."

She spat and pulled her flask from her coat.

"Damn woman," Jack said as Ada handed him the flask for a pull.

"Jist being the way Ah was raised," she shrugged.

"Where was your Pere?"

"Natchez, he cut meat there. My Pa, we was just west of the Atchafalaya," she added.

"Swamp there, right?"

Ada nodded.

Jack side eyed Ada and his eyes became misty.

"No need ta dredge up the past, Mr. Flynn," Ada quickly stated.

"Old Jack is fine." He choked back a swig on Ada's flask. "I knew your Pa."

She patted his back. "Ahmma make it right one day, don't you worry." Ada said as she stared off into the distance and became lost in thought.

CHAPTER FOUR

A fat golden sun sank heavy to the west. Winds and breezes paused and let the stars come out.

Ada sat for several long hours after the sun went down while sharpening her knife. All of her knives were sharp enough to split the hair on a toad four ways. Ada had shot a couple of rabbits earlier in the day. Every muscle and sliver of fat was cut, sliced, and salted, and the bones were boiled. She wasted nothing.

As a child, it was the days after a butchering was when she thought the house smelled the best. Rendered tallow, bone brothers, blood sausage, fresh hide stretched and drying by the door. . . she could still picture it all. Ada felt truly content and at peace on those days. They closed in around her, providing safety and comfort. Night was quiet and filled with peaceful dreams of her past home.

The following day Ada found herself delivering a calf. The sun crossed the sky from the darkest hours before dawn and all the way up to midday as she worked getting the foal out. The heifer had carried without issue, but was sprawled out and filled the valley with her exhausted cries. Ada had risen that morning to the bellows of the mother; Ada knew the birth was close and so was ready as she rode out in the darkness to work.

Ada's shadow vanished beneath her as the calf finally breached. She squatted and pulled. Muscles straining, mouth agape, and with eyes rolled back and white, the heifer pushed her calf into the world. Ada, with muscles straining and teeth grinding, pulled with all of her might. Emerging in a flood of gore and fluid, the calf emerged into the valley.

Ada sat back on her heels and wiped her brow. She tilted her hat back and her shadow lengthened. The small cow shook and trembled as her mother cleaned her. Ada's eyes drifted across the valley's ridge lines. She almost expected to see the scruffy blue heeler.

There was no dog. Instead, three horses with three riders had their eyes upon on her valley.

Acidic rage rose within Ada like bile. She flushed with anger and jumped up into the saddle. She had her rifle free of its scabbard as she rode hard at the strangers. Her war cry filled the previously silent valley as Ada's eyes went red and wild.

The three men sat upon the eastern ridge, apparently too stunned to ride or raise a greeting. As Ada closed the distance, she could see the surprise play across their faces.

Ada became a thundering force in the valley. She fired a shot as she rode and, over one hundred yards away, struck the ridge between the men.

The men's horses pinned and turned. As one the three horses raced off and took their riders with them. Spurring on their mounts, the riders lit a shuck for town.

Between her run-in the with the Preacher in town and the birthing of the calf, Ada was raw. None of the men on the ridge had been him, but she was wary and not willing to take chances. Their eyes on her, and her valley, lit a fire in her that had nearly burned itself out.

Her rifle was ready; she had honed her dead eye and quick reflexes, keeping rattlers dead while protecting cattle. Any outfit she rode for had her ride point due to her skills. She was an ace when hunting from her saddle , and these strangers were obviously unaware of just how much of a disadvantage they were at.

Her gut said ride, so Ada did just that. As she crested the ridge, she put her eye to her scope. The clean outfits and clean horses told her the men were not men in need. They bolted like men aware of their guilt.

Her eyes strayed down to the ground where they'd been watching. Glinting in the fading light was a brass tool lost by one of the strangers.

Ada stepped down from her saddle. Carefully, she lifted and turned over the object. As the soft metal caught the light, a shot rang out in the valley. The echo punctuated the shot before the silence that followed.

Peering towards the setting sun, Ada scanned the opposite end of the valley.

Nothing moved in the growing shadows.

Ada looked down over her cattle and detected no further disturbances.

Settling back in her seat, Ada started for her home at a much slower pace than she had set out from. She noticed the dog crossing the small creek. He was coming up the valley slowly and weaving through the shadows.

Ada swung down and collected cow chips for her hearth, keeping one wary eye on the direction taken by the stray.

She was exhausted and lost herself in thought while collecting the dried manure. "Time fer a flatbed upgrade," Ada said to the roan as she filled the burlap sack tied to his horn. Ada was always forced to make do with too little. Her saddle bags were not made for cords of wood or cow chips. All she had were a few makeshift bags meant to meet her needs. "You wouldn't smell like shit if I had a small wagon, boy." Ada patted the roan as led him back to the stable with their small load of fuel.

The shot concerned her. Natives from the outlands and hunters from town occasionally skirted her valley, but the timing seemed uncanny to her. Ada had just run off the strangers, yet there was no sign of anyone else. That shot had come from the western ridge behind her.

Her nerves already raw from the day, she could not puzzle it out any further. Exhausted as she was, tonight there would be little sleep.

Time and again Ada squinted past the flickering firelight and into the distant darkness. It'd probably been some hunter running a deer, she thought reasonably. As the sun dipped further, Ada brushed and picked the roan in her nightly ritual.

Her thoughts were far away and her mind wandered. It settled on the shimmering red blood of her loved ones pooling on the dusty floorboards. She ached to see them again. It was the only hurt she struggled with.

She wept softly in the dark.

The horse yanked its leg and stomped. In her distraction, Ada had dug too deep into his frog.

"Awe, sorry boy," she said, patting the roan's warm haunch. "Ya good thing, ya are. Ah won't leave ya, we are tied up togeth'r." She wiped her arm across her face and it came away wet. "Ah'll fight with all my bone and blood. Whatever it takes." Her eyes filled with water at the memory of her brother, as she quoted him. He had said these things whenever they sat around the stove and heard their parents worrying about their farm or family.

Arden always had hope. In a world of wet mud, war, and poverty, he'd held onto hope. Ada sat in the stall with her back to the wall. He had been her best and only friend. Her body shook as she cried. She took a long pull from the flask while waiting for the hurt to dull.

The day had taken a toll on Ada. She put a low flame on by the house and made coffee. Ada kept the blaze small and partially blocked the light with a large stone. She dragged her bedding outside and into the darkness just beyond the flame's light. She left the doors open so that if she had to take cover, she could do so in a hurry. For a time she admired the flames, drank coffee, and listened to the night. She cast her gaze toward the heavens and thought more about Arden .

Across her vision from cheekbone to cheekbone stretched the eternal sky full of stars, gasses, and swaths of blackness. She could only look for a brief moment before she began feeling overwhelmed by it all. It wasn't fear that turned her. It was the awe and bewilderment she felt cascading over her mind like a waterfall.

"Too damn much," she muttered before squeezing her eyes closed and putting her face on her saddle. The leather gently creaked under her fingers and she fell into sleep. Every day she felt more torn between settling down and seeking revenge. Not a moment went by that she was not pulled in different directions.

Chapter Five

A gentle breeze stirred the pre-dawn air. The darkness ebbed as the warmth slowly returned to the land. In the pale glow of a new day, Ada found that she was not alone.

Laying at the other side of the remains of the hearth fire was the blue healer. His matted fur glistened and was bloody.

Ada looked around. Not seeing anything else amiss, she rose. She approached cautiously and intentionally. A low growl from the dog held her in place.

Ada bypassed the wounded dog. There was some leftover rabbit drying in her home. Ada retrieved two rough bowls and sat out the rabbit with some water. She crossed over to the roan's stall and pulled her out her tack. The horse did not need the brushing, but it helped her think.

"Dog musta caught tha bullet last night," she whispered to the horse. From where she stood, Ada could just make out where he was shot. She mucked the stall as the dog ate a little.

Even though she knew he was hurting, she noted that the dog made no sound.

Mucking the stall complete, Ada returned to the glowing embers in the pit.

The dog didn't growl.

Thirty minutes passed as Ada drank coffee and watched the valley while also keeping an eye on the dog. Standing slowly, she walked over to the blue heeler.

He laid down and relaxed at her approach and let her check his wound. The bullet had passed straight through him. Whoever had shot the dog had missed his vitals. It was a lucky strike for the dog on a bad shot. He had no shattered bones and he was not bleeding out.

Ada cleaned dressed the wound and got him some more rabbit. Today, she decided to stay close. There was work that had been waiting for William that she could take care of.

The dog slept in the shade of the building by the ashes and coals while Ada tended to her vegetable garden and worked over her water routes to clean them out.

Deciding against working on the smokehouse, she set to sharpening all of her tools instead. She sharpened her tools with great care using a whetstone that she'd purchased from a storekeeper in Hot Springs. The work was slow and methodical as the blades were slowly scraped to a fine sharpness. Eventually every blade and tool she had was cleaned, sharpened, and greased.

Ada's eyes eventually settled on Mary's skillet. It had carried her through many years after leaving home and was one of Ada's few keepsakes. She greased the skillet and lit a popping fire. Once the flames and heat were right, Ada placed the skillet in the pit to cure. As the grease started smoking and curled off into the distance, she sat and thought about the journey that had brought her to this valley.

After the death of her family, she had hunted the Preacher without success. Through that, she had come across many a town sheriff's wanted posters and bounties. There was no shortage of desperate scoundrels after the war. Desperate men rendered desperate deeds, putting themselves outside the law.

She found her tracking skills useful in hunting them, her talents not limited to following footprints or listening for gossip. Good money had been made, along with many enemies, although deputies and sheriffs often did not see her as more than a girl whose place they thought was not to be out hunting bounties.

Many tried to talk her out of it, but, in time, she developed a thick skin and quick wit. Often she would take a job that the lawmen did not expect her to return from. Ada had been scarred by the Preacher and he had instilled in her a deep cynicism and distrust of people. Hunting bounties had also left other hidden scars.

As a child, she had known few men. Joel, his father, Mary's father, and her brother were her whole life. The men she hunted were entirely different. Ada stalked murders, rapists, arsonists, horse thieves, robbers, and other malcontents. These men had opened her eyes to more cruelty and evil than she ever thought existed. She knew the Preacher was evil, but there was so much more than just him in the world.

Ada had an eye for detail that allowed her to always find whatever and whoever she sought. The Preacher had been the exception to this.

"Maybe Ah'd been too hungry for revenge," she whispered to the gray smoke that faded above her. "Maybe that changed a person's instincts."

His darkness had eluded her across the country. She had spent so much of her life on that failed hunt. She never imagined that she would be settling down. It happened by accident.

Ada spent time working as a ranch hand whenever there was a shortage of wanted men. As a woman, she had to constantly prove herself and worked harder and longer hours than most. Other hired hands always watched her and waited for her to fail, but she disappointed them by doing her job well. Occasionally, there would be some trouble when a hand tested her. Ada had learned to box and would quickly lay them out and move on with her work.

Vouched for by wire by the previous outfits she'd worked for, Ada secured a bank loan. It'd been so many years since he had surfaced that Ada had figured the Preacher for dead. Ada imagined him swinging from a tree somewhere with only buzzards for company. Ada started to feel lost and without direction.

She rode herd and eventually ended up in New Mexico. Everything was peaceful and none of the townies looked twice at her. The local natives rode her over to Jack Flynn's valley and the two got along well. They shared a meal and coffee, and the next day they rode into town to see Mr. Guilford about the land. She was good for the money and had a chunk already saved. However, she had not bought land before. Her heart raced at the memory. She remembered how much Joel had loved to farm.

She recalled sitting at the banker's desk. At the time, Ada was sweating and anxious. She shifted her weight and knocked her boots. It took a lot for her to sit in the bank office.

"Surely prefer hogtying a runner to sit'n in that office," she thought as Jack and Ada sat and waited for the wire from her bank in Louisiana to come through.

The banker sat and studied her. Jack Flynn, he knew. Ada Picou, he could not make sense of.

She flushed when he suggested another bank in another town. Ada thought he was looking down his nose at her. When the wire came through, he changed in every way. He was nearly tripping over himself to get her signature. The loan was small;   she and Mr. Flynn had worked out a good deal. She saved a good bit and was able to get Hereford stock.

There were buildings she could order from Mr. Carter's general goods store that were made with all pre-cut timber. It was there she met William.

Like Mr. Flynn, the two were at ease with one another. William showed her the catalog that had the house and told her it was true and she could order one. "See here, Miss Picou," he had pointed to the picture, "it's real."

Ada gave a slight chuckle, "Ah ain't orderin anythin like that; it looks like a toy." The idea humored her, but she could not comprehend it. Instead, she decided to build a small stone cabin.

William met her in the valley and carried stone with her. For months they scoured the area for stones out to the utmost fringes of the valley. Their horses carried whatever they couldn't lift. She started wishing for that wagon already back then. Ada thought to make a small sled, but lacked materials. The process was painfully slow, but she enjoyed the work.

Ada was caught up by Mr. Flynn, Mr. Guilford, and William as they saw her in a different light. To them she was no bounty hunter or desperate daughter of a murdered family.

"You look like one of them pioneers," William pointed out one day, and Ada punched him in the arm with a slight smile.

Ada looked around in the dim moving light cast by the flames at the spot they had selected. They had dug out the earth by a cut under the western ridge where the creek meandered near and the earth wall cast a pleasant shadow.

After digging a large enough area, stones were cracked and placed for a floor. Day after day they loaded sacks with river stones of varying sizes. They also lugged sand up from the banks to pack it all together. At night she tamped the floor with a driving mallet she had found by a railway in Kansas. Once the foundation was settled and firm, they started on walls. Here, she remembered, they ran into a problem.

There was not much in the way of large stones in the area, and the few they found they had to carry back from the desert. Ada remembered William riding the valley and the surrounding area without luck for ages. They had scoured the nearby countryside and had already collected what they could.

At that time, she recalled William stood scratching his head and looking defeated.

Ada stepped into her saddle and said, "Riding ta town, be back in a few."

William nodded, "I'll get to work on that garden," he answered back as she spurred the roan and rode off out of sight.

Ada returned with sticks of dynamite wrapped in cloth. The next day, she placed the sticks in holes and cracks in the rock wall.

William gave a her a wary look.

"Done it all before, ain't the first time Ah blowed stuff up," she said as she sized up her placement. The site was near neither the house, nor the horse. She detonated the dynamite with a whoop and a holler, and boulders and rocks of all sizes and shapes were her reward.

"Won't have ta go lookin no more," she said. She patted the red roan on the neck and walked with William over to the fresh rubble.

The work on the homestead cleared Ada's mind. There were fewer and fewer thoughts of the Preacher as her home came up. Sometimes a day would pass and she would realize she had not thought of him. Those days she felt guilt for living her life for anything but revenge. Her self-chosen mission had been to avenge the deaths of her loved ones.

In contrast, not a day went by that she did not think about Joel, Mary, and Arden. Ada imagined her family working by her side and remembered them all in great detail. Joel's cracked and thick nails, his coarse knuckles, and his sweat. Mary's aroma and how she moved through the world. They worked together in harmony in her mind's eye.

Arden, who would've been around William's age now, she imagined drenched in sweat and with a smile on his face. Ada wondered for the umpteenth time how had she survived. What had spared her the cut of the Preacher's blade?

Ada walked over to the home in the darkness. William had still not returned. He had framed the doors, she thought as she rested her hand upon one. In this way, their house had grown. It truly felt like home. It was not only her blood in these walls.

Ada unrolled her bed and settled down to sleep.

Ada cottoned to most animals. The dog took to her and, after he healed followed by a few weeks of slow going, he joined her on the herd.

William had returned from Mr. Carter's store and the three worked well together. The dog dove through the smut grass and kept the strays in the herd. The cattle were less accepting of the blue heeler than Ada. None ran from him; instead, they just stood alert and watched.

"Where did you come across him," William nodded his head toward the blue heeler.

"He jist showed up," she answered. "Somebody had shot 'im, so he decided ta stay."

William nodded. "I like you, you ugly thing," William said as the dog let William pat his head.

The herd seemed to respect the dog. They each knew their role; the blue heeler kept the cattle rounded up and the cattle followed his lead without straying.

"He must'a come from a ranch or somethin," Ada told William. "He's too natural with it." Ada and the dog, both wild and alone, had found something in the valley that they needed.

Ada eyed William as he worked the smokehouse. When he noticed her eyes on him, he gave a her big smirk and he neck turned a little red.

"Why ya all red, William," she hollered, "you mighty hot, huh?" She gave a soft chuckle and went back to cleaning her rifle.

William grumbled as he sat on the stone floor with a smile on his face.

The three strangers that Ada had run off rode into town. They stabled their exhausted horses went into the bar. The boy working the stable was just dozing off in the shade when they rode in.

"These horses are filthy," he observed. "Poor horses," he said as he removed the saddles and led them to the stalls. He loved animals; they were kind, like him. Each horse was brushed slowly and thoroughly and given hay. Nobody had paid extra for it, but he gave the animals alfalfa because he had a good heart.

CHAPTER SIX

The three men sat at the bar nursing whiskeys and sour about their bruised pride. They knew their employer was going to be angry.

"She wasn't going to shoot us," one ventured.

"You sure of that," asked another.

"I didn't sign up for to die out here, I have a wife back home," added the other, taking drink.

The three men looked related and hangdog. All were tall and thin. They each had light brown hair edged with faint gray. Their eyes were blue and each sported a short beard. As they rode hard back into town, they realized one of the riders had lost his Gurley Transit. It was rare and expensive this far from Texas.

"That transit is going to take weeks and over a month's wages to replace," cursed one of the men.

"Go on back and fetch it," said one of the others. "I'll give my condolences to your wife," he added.

An angry look was exchanged. The debate of whether or not Ms. Picou would have shot them had lasted through the week it took them to navigate themselves back to town once Ada had blown them off course. Setting up camp, they questioned each other over and over. Each had seen the rifle and had heard the rapport after being run off.

She did look angry and fierce, they all agreed. Only one of the three men thought she would have spared them.

That shot they had heard convinced the others that turning tail had been wise. Three drinks in, and many curses later, Mr. Minger entered the room.

Mr. Minger was a tall at six foot five inches and was a lean man. Muscular and narrow, he moved with a languid flow that belied his speed. He wore a cap over his short black hair. He strode to the bar with an ominous presence. He looked over the bar room and his piercing gaze settled on the three men drinking with their faces down as they avoided his eyes.

"You three Burman brothers, what say you," he asked in a businesslike manner while sauntering over to the bar,. A filthy city of coal and iron had shaped him and spit him out and his eyes were shrewd, cruel, and missed nothing. "What went wrong," he asked.

The three brothers knew they should not have accepted his land surveying proposal. He had a reputation, and Minger had seen in the brothers exactly what he was looking for. They were weak and needed him more than he needed them.

Leaning back against the bar, he sized the brothers up. Hiring these surveyors had cost him a good bit, and he was ready for his return. He was going to get either his money's worth out of them, or their hides.

"She shot at us," one blurted.

The other two jumped in talking over each other.

"What about the maps," Minger asked.

The three brothers stumbled over each other as they made their excuses.

Minger eventually raised an open palm and silenced them. He towered over the brothers and his intense gaze stilled their voices. His finger drifted to the first brother closest to him. "Mr. Burman, you signed a contract. You committed yourself to this job," Reginald Minger continued, "I expect that you were able to perform you duty."

"She rode on us hard," the first brother said with his eyes on the floor. "There was hellfire in her eyes," he explained, "she had a rifle on us."

Minger was quiet and unmet expectations hung in the air between them.

"We did not get the measurements, sir," the brother finally answered.

In a quick and smooth motion Minger had his gun out that was tied down on his crisp blue jeans. He looked like a cowboy in a painting. Everything about Minger was sharp. Barrel tilted, he shot the speaking brother in the foot.

The other two brothers fell alongside him as the one who was shot collapsed.

Gun now holstered, Minger threw back a shot of whiskey left behind on the counter. He silently met the eyes of each man. "Get that map done," he stated clearly, "or next time I'll aim higher. All three of you will go back East in boxes.. Do you want that for your families?" Reginald Minger put money on the counter and took a bottle of whiskey as he walked toward the door. "Don't fail me gentlemen; I will not suffer it."

The three men and the small group of patrons watched him leave in deafening silence.

Minger was a foul and cunning man that the townies didn't dare approach. He stalked through the town as though on a mission. He never lingered or made small talk with anyone. Back in the big cities he had been a shark, and here he saw himself as a wolf. Out here he stayed hungry for riches and found himself driven by the promise of opportunity. Only the land itself would satisfy him now; he saw in it wealth that he could never acquire in Boston or Chicago. In time, he would own it all and he would squeeze the land for all that it was worth.

"None of these backward yokels stand a chance," spat Minger, "Picou included."

CHAPTER SEVEN

Ada always carried extra rounds either in her bandoleer or saddle bags. Right now, she figured that she would only need one bullet. Before she went back to town to hunt the Preacher, she wanted to stock her larder, so she and the dog were hunting.

The dog and Ada rode the length of the valley along the eastern ridge and headed north. They settled in a grassy glade where she wanted to test him with rabbits.

Using a bow and arrow, she shot five hares that the dog ran. Ada had learned to use a bow well from her Pere. It was the only weapon Mary permitted her to hunt with as a child.

The dog took naturally to running rabbits.

Ada called the dog back and heard the deer nearby before she saw them. They came through the brush and made only a soft rustle. Gentle as it was, it stood out as a sound different from everything else on the glade. She got down on one knee and had her rifle up and ready in a heartbeat.

It only took one shot. One deer fell and the rest scattered.

Ada flicked her hand and the dog ran to the kill. She whistled for the roan and it clopped toward her before it stopped a few feet away. He pawed the ground and chuffed.

This horse did not like blood. She watched as he stood loyally by despite his fears. She tied the deer's legs together and laid it behind the saddle.

"What am Ah," she thought. "Not much a rancher," she surmised. "A retired bounty hunter, almost." "Who was Ah," she questioned.

Ada's father had spun tales of the western frontier and was a lover of stories. Mary did not approve, but both children listened in rapt attention and were always hungry for more. Joel talked a lot by the light of the stove fire. It was the only time he talked, aside from church work. He talked of his father, the butcher of the congregation. The only topic he skirted was the war. If anything did arise of the war that tore the country apart, Mary quieted that talk quickly, and Joel would soon lose himself in the dancing flames.

Ada and Arden would head to bed if Joel mentioned the war. It was a side of him they did not understand. However, they would never go to bed on their own if he mentioned the lands beyond the Mississippi. The stories of the expansion and territories were the ones Ada loved the most. It was a wide and open land where anything was possible. The territories, to her, were opportunities for adventure and exploring. They called to her. Like to like, raw and untamed lands that they were. The tug at her soul never ebbed and she knew one day she'd find her home out there.

Ada methodically field dressed the deer and the hares. The meats were cut thin, salted, and hung to dry in the small house.

During these times, she often thought about William and the smokehouse, but that seemed far away. "It would be nice," she said to no one. William was not around when she came back with the venison and cony. There was a spot cut into the eastern ridge not twenty yards from the home where they had started the addition. She had sized up that spot for a while and they had decided it would be ideal.

Ada threw the dog a hoof and the dog happily chewed the rest of the day away. Water came to a boil on the hearth and was ready for making the bone broth.

When Ada and William built the house, they had added dried storage in the walls and floor. There were small alcoves under stone slabs packed tight with salt, which was abundant here. She had stumbled across an old salt mine—shallow, and mostly depleted save for a few veins—on the north end of her land. She did not know how deep the veins ran, but what was there and what they could get to satisfied their needs. The density of salt kept plants and insects away from inside the home, and they never had weeds or bugs coming through the cracks.

She thought back on Joel's stories.

"When Rome sacked Carthage," her father had once said, "they razed everything and salted the earth so nothing would grow."

Ada had enjoyed the stories of war a great deal and was proud of the home she helped build.

Salt did bring unforeseen challenges. Ada and William shared a home free of pests and weeds, but, that salt caused problems for metals. The lower door hinges looked as though they belonged on an ocean ship. They were new purchased from Mr. Carter, but looked ancient. Loose salt always found a way onto the hinges, and the only recourse was to constantly keep the metal in the home well oiled. Any rendered animal fat they had was used on those hinges.

"So long as they worked," Ada thought.

After taking care of the food and greasing the door hinges, Ada used the remaining grease to soften her saddle. She rubbed the grease into the leather and worked it for the remaining hours of the day. The dog softly whined, the hoof long gone.

Ada threw him another. He had earned it.

Tail wagging, the dog scooped it up and took it to a shady spot in the stall. Ada whistled as she worked. Her and her brother had shared a whistling game. One sibling would pick up where the other left off, and a tune would start, pause, and get picked up again while occasionally changing in tone and timbre.

Remembering this game had her thinking back on Arden's short life.

"Moven through our days like a steam locomotive," she thought. "Blood pumps and pushes us. A leak leads ta a dead stop."

Arden was young and bothersome, but generally had good ideas. He would puzzle over ways to move water, which was something Joel was passionate about. Her brother thought about things like crop rotations to avoid depleting the soil.

Joel, as a result, used Arden's ideas to move water out from the pasture and rotated the family's crops. Water, something they had to have, was also their biggest enemy. Too much in the field caused rot and made hooves soft, the infections in a swamp were almost impossible to treat. The animals of course needed it, but only to drink, not to wallow in.

Father lost few head from time to time due to their becoming lame. He was diligent despite the hardship and worked to drain the land and keep the crop rotation up. Swales and ditches helped divert the water and control it, somewhat. It was a constant battle against nature to raise enough crops and livestock to keep the family fed and in their home.

"All his ideas vanished when his steam let out," thought Ada as she pictured the Preacher in Mr. Guilford's office. Her fists clenched and she bit her jaw.

CHAPTER EIGHT

Riding into town, Ada was sour and ached over the memories of her family. The dog had started to follow, but Ada didn't want that.

"They don't got stables for dogs, stay," she said as she threw him a femur she had held off boiling the day before. The dog accepted the offering and stayed put.

It took a few days to ride to town. There were no open roads she could race down, just weaving paths across varied terrain. There was a stream by the town, probably why the town was built in this spot. She could give the roan his head and he would always go to water. It was slow going and she was anxious to find the Preacher. She wore an extra bandoleer and an extra belt for both bullets and knives. Ada was armed for war as she rode steady and slept little.

A calm washed over her and she felt like the end of something was near.

Ada rode the roan into the stable.

The stable boy looked admiringly at the horse as Ada turned him over. "Brush'm down, give'm hay and water, and check his hooves, wouldjya?" Ada tossed the boy the coin for the roan's lodging.

"Gracias," the boy shouted joyfully. He was small for his age and had a bright white smile that spread from ear to ear. Ada had noticed him before and saw how much he enjoyed working with the animals and so was happy to leave her roan in his care.

As she crossed the street to Mr. Carter's general goods store, Ada nodded to the townspeople. Heads turned to her, but she noted fewer nods. It had not been that long ago that she had shot up the town's law office, so she expected this cooler reception. However, she had not been run out of town, yet. It was a good sign.

Sheriff Pile was on his stoop and gave her a wave. "Morning Miss Ada," he added, "hope you aren't looking for trouble." He eyed her gear and tilted his head back. "Ma'am are you looking for war," he asked.

"Nah, just lookin t'do yer job," she threw a fake smile at him. "Ya git that varmint lock'd up yet?'

"Hasn't been in town since you ran him off, Miss Picou."

She huffed and changed direction. "Those surveyors 'round?" she asked the sheriff.

"Not sure, Miss Picou," he answered, "are you hunting them too?" She smirked, "jist return'n their shit." She walked into Mr. Guilford's office and found that he was out.

She left the surveyor's tool on his desk. If anyone knew where the Preacher was, it would be William. He had been spending extra time recently in Mr. Carter's store, and everyone on the frontier needed supplies. Mr. Carter's was the only store around. It took her eyes a moment to adjust to the dimmer indoor light.

She saw William waiting on a stranger.

"Hey, Ada," William nodded to her and smiled once he saw her.

She nodded back.

The stranger tensed, but relaxed in a moment.

Ada's attention now drawn, she looked him over. Man looked like a city tenderfoot to her eye. She side eyed him and noted that his clothes were new and there was little wear at the cuffs. The boots were still stiff as he walked and appeared like they had not been broken in. She stood, monetarily confused, and with her brow furrowed. He smelled like flowers, but she did not see flowers on him. Ada knew of perfume and had crossed paths with working women who used it. It was not faint though, and it was not on him from a tryst.

As she puzzled over this, two men came into the store. Ada did not notice them as she was focused on the strange man. She was behind the door by the pepper and coffee making her selections and they did not see her either.

The stranger turned and faced the men. "Gentlemen," he greeted them with a looming stare.

"Mr. Minger," the men said, shifting nervously. "We will head back out there," one of the men said.

The other blurted out, "but I need my tools."

"We know you want the map done, but my brother cannot ride as of now," one of the surveyors shifted uncomfortably.

Reginald Minger stood at the counter with a box in his hand. There was a heavy silence weighing down the floorboards.

Ada realized who the two men where. Turning to the man that had spoken first, she said, "Ah put yer damn tool on Mr. Guilford's desk. Fetch it if need be, but don't trespass again." She then turned to Minger and added, "What the hell are ya doin sendin folk to my land," her voice getting louder by the moment.

William put the box down and reached under the counter for Mr. Carter's shotgun.

Minger put his hands up and gave an oily smile. "We were just collecting some information for a map of the territory. I own the land adjacent to yours; deeply sorry for any misunderstandings," he finished with a smile that did not touch his eyes. "Please, please, let me buy you a drink." He stood with his arms open in a welcoming gesture. "You and I can talk business without these idiots sullying things." He nodded his head at the two surveyors. "Didn't Miss Picou tell you where you could find your precious equipment?"

"Yes, sir, we'll be off then," one of the men said. The two men nearly ran out the store.

"So, Miss Picou, what about that drink," Minger asked.

Ada laughed dryly. "No, Ah don't think so, Chicago. I'll take daft of my brew elsewhere. Ya keep yer hired help off my land; otherwise, Ah might shoot ya all dead," she finished as she put her thumbs through her belt of weapons.

The tension in the air was like the buzz before the storm. Muscles everywhere drew taut.

Minger backed down gracefully. "Miss Picou, you are right madam." He collected the rest of his purchases from the counter. "There was no business us being there. We will let you be." In exaggerated tones he added, "Best of luck to you in all of your endeavors." With that, he left the store, package in hand.

Just as William returned the shotgun back under the counter, Ada shouted after Minger, "Ah 'ppreciate ya all not comin uninvited."

William looked at her and shook his head. "I think they were invited," William said.

"What tha hell are ya talkin 'bout," asked Ada.

"I think that man, Reginald Minger, hired them to survey out by our place."

"They ain't welcome," she growled.

"Yeah, we'll have to keep an eye on those fellas," observed William.

They both stood in silence as they watched Reginald Minger saunter to his wagon before heading over the bar.

"That was a sight," William said with a nervous laugh.

"Stow it, William," Ada said quickly, but still smiling. "Ah wonder who that man was and why he hired surveyors ta put eyes on my land."

William shifted uneasily. "'Our land,' don't you mean?"

"Yea, sorry William, jist hot right now," Ada said dismissively.

William loaded her a box of supplies and said, "Well, I know why he sent them. Mr. Guilford told me that out-of-towner is buying up land all over. Well, at least he's trying to. Apparently folk around here are not taking to him. He was all over Old Jack before you came out here, but Mr. Flynn wouldn't sell that land to Mr. Minger. Said it was a family heirloom, all he had left, he told him."

"He never said that ta me," Ada toed her boot in thought.

"Everyone wondered for a while if you were his kin," William shrugged. "Mr. Guilford set them right, told them you were a friend and to mind themselves. Old Jack said you were 'good people.' He told Mr. Guilford he knew Picous from the Mississippi Delta.."

Ada was hit hard by this news. Her chest tightened.

"Mr. Guilford would know more of course, but he is buttoned up pretty tight, he never airs other folks business."

No longer in the mood for such business, Ada finally asked what she had come to town for. "Have ya seen the blue-eyed man Ah shot in tha office?" She bit her lip.

"Sorry, Ada I haven't. I've been watching and asking around. I stayed around for a while to scout, but nobody knows where he went after you ran him off."

Ada hung her head and released her fists. "Alright then, Ah'm going ta grab a bite 'fore Ah ride out."

"Maybe something will turn up," William added quickly.

Ada noted the hope in his voice, maybe a bit of pity as well.

"That's a bit moren I've heard ya say in a while William."

He turned red and shifted to get the beans from Ada's list.

"Ah'll have ta see Mr. Guilford 'fore Ah light out," she said. "Ya know, yer 'good people' too William. Ah'll see ya back at tha house and give tha dog another bone when ya get there."

William looked confused. "The dog?"

Ada had already left and was carrying her supplies to the stable.

William stood for a while thinking on Ada Picou. He hoped the law could catch the man that killed her family; he could see it eating her from the inside. "She deserves some peace," William said to himself. She was the best part of this territory as far as he was concerned.

Ada walked with steady strides to the boarding house after dropping the provisions and supplies off with the stable boy. She took in every window and door as she made her way down the main street; she didn't want to be surprised again by the Preacher she hunted.

Instead of walking around the buildings and in obscured areas, she kept herself visible. She thought to draw out that snake, if he was still around. Ada wanted to be ready no matter the direction of the danger.

She made her way into Peace's place— for a meal at the only boarding house in town. The establishment she had started with her husband was clean and simple.

Ms. Peace was a widow of the west, just one member of a group too numerous to count. She was kind and generous, but fierce and tempered by a hard life. Her strength and resilience were what she and Mr. Peace relied on as they crossed the Mississippi and journeyed west. Mr. Peace was a retired Union Army commander who, without a war, looked to tame the untamed. Mr. Peace had led the drive of a few families—including Mr. Carter, the doctor—when word had spread that the Peace's were leaving and making a new life for themselves in a new land not scarred by war.

Ms. Peace occasionally reminisced with Mr. Carter, "my husband only settled down when he died; he was a driven man."

After a bit of panning and stumbling across veins in a river on their route, Ms. Peace was left with a substantial sum and settled in at the town where her husband was buried. There was no push, or pull, that would see Ms. Peace leave her husband's side. Finding the building for sale, she partnered with Mr. Guilford and Mr. Carter and established Peace's Place. The establishment ran smoothly, and almost mechanically. Her only employee was a refugee with a tumultuous history, a Mexican woman named Therese.

Ms. Peace did all of the cooking, and everything else they shared in labor. Therese was young and fearful, but had a fire that Ms. Peace recognized as similar to what was in herself. Therese had not traveled north into New Mexico for the love of adventure or in search of a land to conquer. She, beautiful in feature and character, had run north while being chased by the lust of vaqueros. Together they worked before the sun appeared and long after it departed for the day.

There was no menu at Peace Place. The offerings were eggs, toast, bacon, and grits, either all together or a la carte. There was also occasionally a hot, thick biscuit and butter. Ada was a regular and Ms. Peace had cottoned to her.

"Welcome back Ada," Ms. Peace said from the kitchen window behind a small bar.

"Good ta be among the livin," Ada sat at small table close to the bar.

"Therese just made a fresh pot," Ms. Peace said a good natured tone as the girl brought Ada some coffee.

"Much obliged," Ada tipped her hat and spotted a little red creeping up Therese's neck.

"Therese, come grab this plate," hollered Ms. Peace.

Therese darted away and soon returned with breakfast.

"Well, Ah'll be," Ada grinned.

"Toad in a hole," Ms. Peace said with a smile while leaning in from the kitchen.

"Thank ya mightily mam," offered Ada.

Ms. Peace toasted thick slices of bread over butter in the skillet and used a glass to cut a hole in both slices of toast before dropping in the eggs. They were served runny and Ada took her time sopping it all up. Not sure how she was so lucky, she savored her breakfast.

Therese kept her coffee topped off all the while.

Ada turned an eye to Therese and asked "What's this all 'bout?"

"Nada," Therese responded with a shrug.

"You stirred things up a good bit last time you were in town," Ms. Peace said as she came out from the kitchen while wiping her hands on her apron. "I figured people were going to be slow to warm up to you again. Mr. Guilford told me you were collecting on that man. He must've been something awful for you to do as you did in that law office." Ada tensed and Ms. Peace quickly added, "I don't know anything about any of it, but I'm throwing my lot in with you. I've seen you with William, and if Old Jack and Mr. Guilford think kindly of you, well, I don't see any reason I shouldn't."

Ada softened. "Thank ya mam, Ah ain't used ta kindness like this."

"Well quit gabbin and eat up," Ms. Peace nodded and went back to the kitchen. Ada heard the sounds of cooking and couldn't help a small smile playing across her face.

Ada ate slower than she usually did. She took her time and savored every bite while enjoying the meal. This was something more than food: It was thoughtfulness she needed to think on. As Ada sopped up the remains of her eggs with her biscuit, she realized that not only was it the best breakfast she had in a while, but that it could be her last if the Preacher got the drop on her.

Her eyes drifted out into the street and Ada imagined the man with blue eyes and black garb waiting for her. Ada thought about the Preacher and her last encounter in the law office. He had not recognized her after all the years, but undoubtedly he would now. There was a chance that he would be as prepared as she was. This realization did not affect her the way she had thought. There was no tension in her shoulders and her mind was clear. Something about this town and these people gave her courage. As Ada slowly drank her coffee, hot and black, she heard the thundering of hooves approach.

Ada had come to town expecting trouble. She had shot up the law office and crossed paths with the man who killed her family, after all. However, it did not come from the angle she expected. Her rifle was propped by the door, her six-shooters untied. Her belts and bandoleers were heavy with knives and bullets. She had been facing the windows with her back to the kitchen, and saw the riders when they arrived.

Horses and men glistened with sweat in the cloud of dirt that their arrival had churned up. She saw the stirrups, heard the clinking of metal, and saw their wild look. They reared their horses in front of the boarding house.

Behind her there was a gasp and a glass was dropped. It that shattered on the dry wooden floor and sent shards flying in all directions.

Ada turned and saw a ghostly white Therese. She saw the small Mexican woman dive behind the bar followed by the distinct sound of shells being loaded into the late Mr. Peace's MacNaughton shotgun.

"Seems they're ready fer trouble too," thought Ada before turning back to the street.

Ms. Peace came from the kitchen and said, "What in tarnation?" She glanced out the windows before she saw Therese loading the shotgun. "Girl, what in the world are you doing?"

"If ya got a safe place 'round here, git to it." Ada threw a quick nod to Therese, who responded with a knowing look of her own. It was not clear to Ada who these men were. She stayed low and retrieved her rifle from beside the door.

A man's voice boomed heavy and thick with a Spanish accent.

"Ada Picou," he yelled, "you leave here and don't come back!" He continued, "Go back east, go back to your people, we let you live."

Someone else said something in Spanish. Ada knew very little Spanish, as she had only lived near Acadaian French by the Atchafalaya.

Ms. Peace shouted, "Be off you, or I'll get the Sheriff!"

The men ignored her.

Ada threw a questioning look to Therese. The Mexican woman was pale and shaking. Their eyes met, and Therese shook her head.

Ada, with rifle in hand, walked to the door. "Who tha heller y'all s'posed t' be," she asked the group of men.

One man who was larger than the rest and dressed in military garb spat, "I am Alejandro Gaspard, who are you."

"I'm Ada Picou and I ain't goin' nowhere." She leaned in the doorway with the rifle cradled in her arms and at the ready.

The men looked to one another. The leader, chewing on a piece of leather, said, "You must leave this," he spread his arm wide.

Ada chuckled. "Nah hoss, ya can run along now, an 'leave this,'" she mocked.

Someone in the group spoke sharply in Spanish. Alejandro glared at Ada and held his horse still. The air sparked with electricity. Both figures stood like stone statutes, every muscle taut and straining.

Ada heard Therese crack the shotgun beside her.

"You go," Therese yelled while pointing the shotgun at Alejandro. His eyes went wide and the veins in his forehead bulged.

"You—" Alejandro's voice shook with shock and fury. He yelled something in Spanish and a gun went off.

Wood shattered near Therese's head before both women dove back into the dining area.

Upstairs, Ms. Peace kicked open the door to the front balcony. She let fly a roar of gunfire into the crowd below. "You two girls stay low," she yelled. "I told you all to leave!" Ms. Peace yelled over the shots.

Confusion seized the group as a man fell to the ground and his blood pooled atop the sandy roadway.

Ada squeezed off a couple of rounds into the growing dust cloud as Therese slid over to the door frame, took a low position, and fired.

Glass exploded around them. Everything was a blur of motion and sound as the deafening roar of gunfire raged. The fury of a river's rapids made of lead and steel echoed throughout the town.

Ms. Peace was struck by a bullet from below and let out a cry. "Run, girls!" Ms. Peace gasped while holding her bleeding wound.

Therese was also bleeding from a wound in her arm that was studded with wood splinters.

Bullets flew from the many pistols wielded by the many men.

There seemed to be no end to the amount of lead flying through Peace's boarding house.

Half of the men reloaded while others continued firing. The glass in the windows was mostly gone, and the floor and tables were splintered and pocked with bullet holes.

Ada had overturned a thick table and was perched behind for shelter. The table was being chewed apart by the rounds coming in. Rifle spent, Ada now leaned on her six-shooters.

"Ya goddamn sonsabitches," Ada yelled as spit and blood flew from her lips.

The acrid smell of gunpowder stung her nose and the dust that was kicked up burned her eyes. She could make out Therese still firing and reloading, although shells were nearly spent. She was blood-soaked, but steady in her movement.

The two women had heard Ms. Peace's yells along with the sound of her fall. Ada knew she had shot a few men, yet the dust cloud did not diminish in size. They were firing blind and the steady hail of bullets continued without any sign of easing up.

"Out of shells," Therese rolled toward Ada and hid behind the table. She was bleeding. "They have come to kill me," she yelled in English over the cacophony. "It is all my fault," Therese wailed, "it is my fault we will all die."

"Nah," shouted Ada, "they'r ask'n fer me." She did not know why they wanted her to go or who they were, but she was angry and that anger fueled her survival instinct.

"We kin git out," she yelled to Therese. She indicated to the hall with her head. "Down that way there's a door, right?"

Therese tensed, knowing what Ada had in mind. There was a lull in the shooting as the men stopped their onslaught.

"Now," yelled Ada. She stood and fired into the wall of dust as they both sprang for the hallway. Those few rounds had given her the moment they needed. Immediately after they had leapt away, a fresh hail of returned bullets shattered the table's top.

"Come on," Ada said. She was nearly blinded by sweat and gore as she crawled on her elbows down the hall. Ada took the occasional shot behind her.

"It's all ruined," Therese groaned as she glanced back at the bullet-riddled room. "Where is Ms. Peace?"

Therese was about to run back to her death, but Ada caught her and held her with strong arms. "Peace's pro'ly dead, we gotta go," Ada tried consoling Therese. "There ain't nothin ya can do now; we gotta run like Peace said."

They made it to the back door and Ada took a quick glance outside. No one was out back.   Together she and Therese dove for the ditch running behind the false-faced town.

The sun was getting low and cast a shadow across their sprawled bodies. Both Therese and Ada panted and scraped the sweat out of their dust-caked eyes. There clothes were torn and thick with blood.

They made their way through mud and muck as the shooting slowed and died away. They could not see the street, but they could hear the men make their way slowly into the building. Soon, they were too far away to hear the curses in Spanish when the men re-emerged empty handed.

Ada's raw fingers twitched while looking for a trigger. The two women crawled and wormed their way through a barbed wire fence that'd been newly raised.

"Watch yerself, stay low." Ada held the lowest wire so Therese could slide under unscathed.

Their only routes went south and east; going north back to Ada's home was impossible, as it would bring them right back through town.

"Away, we gotta git away, as far away as we kin right now." Ada's sharp eyes searched for riders. As soon as they could stand and run, they did. Bleeding and bruised they ran out of town as though they were being chased out by the devil.

The town was well behind them by the time they heard more gunfire.

"What was that," asked Therese.

"Ain't no tell'n," answered Ada. "Pro'ly more killing." There was no time to turn and look.

They had no chance to take her roan, but if they stole a horse, they would hang, so Ada felt secure in leaving him behind.

Ada and Therese ran with all their might. Out beyond town they slid down a bank and through a creek. Panting and sweat drenched, they continued on as their pursuers closed in behind them.

They hid in a low spot in the water And Therese held some loose brambles over them to block the two women from sight. The water was cool in the darkness and felt good on their wounds. Ada held her guns aloft and had her ammo belts around her neck.

"There's a moccasin nest 'round here somewhere." Ada peered around hoping they were not near.

The horses rode by. Once the thunderous sound of hooves faded, the two women continued to flee.

The two put miles between themselves and Ms. Peace's. By the time dawn came, they found that they had reached the lava flows.

"Be wary of yer step," Ada told Therese. "This here rock ain't always what it seems."

They moved with caution and trepidation while seeking shelter. There were many caves and alcoves nearly invisible even to the trained eye and that were made by the black rock as it wove and turned over itself.

"This here black rock looks like frozen waves," Ada mentioned to Therese as she remembered what it looked like in the Gulf of Mexico.

Therese shook her head, not understanding.

Eventually the two stopped running. Totally spent and weary all the way down to their bones, they leaned upon the walls. They followed the cool surface and eventually stumbled across an alcove.

"It looks like the entrance to Satan's domain," said Therese as she made the sign of the cross upon herself.

Ada followed the cave until it stopped. "Damn, we're lucky as hell," Ada swore before tilting back her hat and wiping her brow.

Therese frowned at Ada's words. "Yes, lucky." She toed a small collection of skeletal remains. Water had come from above or below and pooled, forming tracks around it.

"Waters safe ta drink," Ada pointed to the tracks.

"You so sure?" Therese pointed to the dead man.

"Didn't die from this here water, was shot," Ada put a finger through the hole in the man's vest.

They drank deeply and collected themselves. Regardless of the corpse, both Ada and Therese fell into a dead sleep as soon as they were seated. They passed the night with their backs against the cool lava rock.

When they woke and inspected more of their surroundings, they found that the only animal tracks near the spring were from small game.

"This place'll do fer a bit," said Ada as the sun peeked out around mid-day. "Shot grazed ma head," she mumbled to herself while gingerly touching her scalp.

Ada's clothes were torn and ripped in many places. She looked down and saw the blood on her shirt and pants and remembered Therese's wounds. Ada looked over and saw that Therese still slept.

"Come on now, wake up." Ada gave Therese a gentle shake. "Ya've been bleed'n as much as me."

There was blood in Therese's hair and caked on her arm.

"Looks like yer a lucky one." Ada used a torn segment of shirt to gently wipe the blood from Therese's head. "This one, jist missed ya," Ada frowned. She knew not all wounds left marks on the skin. "Yer left arm was hit bad."

The blood on Therese's skin was dry and Ada cleaned the wound and dressed it as well as she could with what little supplies they had. Therese followed Ada's instructions on dressing her head. The bleeding had stopped on its own in the night, but Therese looked deathly pale.

"I just need rest," asserted Therese. "The run was hard."

Ada nodded and sat back on her heels. "Ah'm sure Ah'm a sight as well." "Ah'd say ya done alright for somebody who'd been shot," she gave Therese a gentle pat. "Might better than most folks Ah've known."

Therese gave Ada a feeble smile and closed her eyes.

Therese spent the day weaving in and out of sleep. It had taken well over an hour to get all the wood splinters out of Therese's arm.

"Yer arm's in bad shape. Gotta watch fer infection."

Weary and still covered in blood, they slept. Ada was awakened by Therese trying to get water. Their eyes met and, nodding, Ada got up and used her hat to procure Therese a drink.

Ada took stock as best she could. "They'll be hunt'n us; they lost men," she added. "Nobody shoots off that much unless they gotta stake in somethin."

"Yes," Therese said before looking at the ground.

Ada sat and thought about many things as she tried to clean her guns and checked over her ammunition. "Not much left here," she said as she piled up the remaining bullets in the sand.

"I have nothing," Therese responded.

"The guns a'right, but we ain't got much to shoot with 'em." Ada bit her jaw and looked up at the ceiling in exasperation. "Have to bow hunt if we gonna make it," she said with frustrated finality.

"This I do not know, but I will learn, we will survive, I know it." Therese spoke such hopeful words, yet they dripped with sadness.

"Ms. Peace'll be a'right. The doc in town'll take care," Ada said this for herself as much as Therese.

Therese sighed and looked around with tears in her eyes. "My brother is small and he will be next. I worry for him, and yet I cannot be there for him now." She spoke with heartbreak in her voice; the fleeting hope was gone.

"Yer brother, tends the horses?"

Therese nodded.

"Damnation, what's this all about," Ada slapped her hat against the ground and growled. She stalked off into the night, leaving the cave and Therese behind her while cursing the men who caused all of this.

A few days passed. Both women rested at the edge of the pool, realization dawning as their hunger set in and desperation began to show in both of their eyes. As Ada sat trying to understand what had happened in town, she found that they just did not know what it was all about. The threats and gunfire told one story, but another had to exist.

"Who woulda hired em," Ada asked the wind.

"I have a place we can hide," Therese offered. She was cowing, blaming herself, Ada realized.

Brow furrowed, Ada asked, "Where's that?"

"It's in the north. It be cold, but safe," Therese was drawing a map in the sand as she spoke.

Ada thought about her horse, cattle, and dog. Her home was northeast of town, but Therese wanted to go north and west.

Ada felt a flare of anger. "Ah'm gonna rain fire on 'em," she barked out.

Therese, focused on the map, jumped.

"Sorry." Ada looked at Therese and felt a bit of shame. "Ah'm just hot and Ah'll be damn Ah'm gonna be run off."

Therese nodded and looked into the pool.

"They was Mexicans, right?" Ada said .

Therese nodded again.

"Ah saw the stirrups and heard 'em talkin. The had vaquero saddles," added Ada.

"They were after me; still will be," Therese said quietly.

"They ain't aft'r ya girl, they called me out." Ada sat and looked hard at Therese. "Why you think they want ya?" she asked the dark-haired beauty. She knew the truth in her gut, even when Therese would not answer. "Ya knew 'em," Ada's eyes squinted while watching Therese's body language.

"I did," was all Therese could muster.

After a few minutes of silence, Ada stood.

"We can't stay here; they'll be huntin this way. We didn't cover our tracks." At dusk, Ada went outside and looked back on their trail from atop a great black wave.

In the distance she saw the flicker of a campfire.

"Who'd be this'a way?" Ada asked.

"It is them, I am sure," Therese answered confidently.

The silence of the desert night was broken by gunshots. Both women dove into the sand. After a few more gunshots and no signs of pursuit, they stood.

"Yeah, that's them. Drunk as hell."

Ada considered ambushing them, but she was under powered and Therese would be put into more danger.

Therese scowled.

"Gotta move," Ada told Therese in a tense voice. "Lead on."

Therese followed the North Star and they took a wide berth of town. The two women covered their tracks this time, but they knew it wouldn't do much despite how it slowed them down a great deal.

"It'll keep 'em guess'n." Ada pointed toward some rocky outcroppings as they crossed the softer sand.

They traveled quietly and quickly. In the early gray light of dawn, they came across a creek.

"Hold," Ada motioned to Therese while indicating to a single small fawn. "Must have been separated." She slung the rifle quietly off her shoulder. Ada aimed with steady muscles and an unflinching eye.

The rapport of the bullet bounced all over the creek.

"They heard that fer sure," Ada shouldered the rifle and ran to the fawn. It was small enough to through it over her shoulders.

"I can help," Therese said.

"Not yet, we gotta git, quick." Ada hissed, already running north and west away from the water. Therese and Ada dressed the fawn together once they thought they were far enough away. Tucking themselves into a small earthen outcropping, they made short work of the carcass. They were worried about their pursuers hearing the shot, but the notion of food and supplies that the deer offered far outweighed the fear. They could use all of the skin, meat, and sinew that they could carry between the two of them. The rest had to be left behind.

As Ada scraped the skin clean, Therese worked out the bladder for use as a canteen and sliced the meat thin. The hide was not as well cleaned and stretched as Ada would have preferred, but still, she said, "this'll have ta do fer now." She frowned at the remains and looked to the sky. Buzzards would be here soon and would attract unwanted attention.

"There's only so much we can do," Therese said as she looked around nervously.

Ada quickly made a satchel as best she could from the raw skin. She held it up and inspected the rough work. "Won't hold much, it'll do fer now." She kept anything that could be useful on the run and left the rest in the hollow. They threw a bit of sand and dirt to cover what was left. "Won't keep the scavengers away," Ada observed.

Therese nodded.

"A'right, let's go, Ah'm sure that shot's drawn 'em in a mite."

"We go north," Therese said, leading the way.

Together, they continued north and out of sight of the town. Every night they saw the low light of a far-off camp behind them.

"It's doggin us," Ada said as she looked out into the darkness with her eyes set on the distant flames. "They ain't gonna run us down," she said, clenching her jaw and flexing her fists. She cast a worried eye back onto Therese who was sitting in the dirt and hugging her knees.

They took shifts as lookouts and over time found patterns that worked for them. They stayed alert during their journey north. It took a toll on both women, but neither would relent. Every dark shadow they saw from the corner of their eyes belied a hidden threat.

"Tha seasons turn'n," Ada said upon noting a chill in the wind one morning. It was slight, only a few degrees, but enough to mark the coming of winter. "Winter'll be ease'n in soon, Ah hope we're git'n close," Ada's said with her eyes on Therese.

The small glowing spot of light reappeared every night. It was following them apace. Ada swore at every sunset, hoping but never satisfied to find that it would be gone.

"They ain't let'n up seems." Ada sat on her heels while carving at a stick. "Don't know where we are though, jest that we're head'n north. They ain't as dumb as they look." Ada threw the stick in the darkness.

"They will have scouts. We are not leaving much of a trail," Therese looked at her feet. They were bloody and sore, she had lost her sandals in the creek.

Ada and Therese covered their trails as best they could and rarely lit a campfire. When they did light one, it was along a south-facing embankment. The embers were kept weak and they scattered the smoke with green sticks as trees were getting more common.

Making their way north, they had crossed over from hardy brush to small shrubs, then the small shrubs gave way to trees. The colors of the area become a richer and more verdant green. However, there were also more wolves.

"They gonna be a problem," Ada observed as a pack of wolves far ahead of them made their way east.

"A problem for another day," Therese added, "if that day comes." She looked brokenhearted to Ada's eyes. A pang of guilt shot through Ada as she thought on how she had caused so much ruin in town by just being there.

Ada had not fired a shot since the deer by the creek. Therese had been foraging to supplement the venison for as long as it would last.

"We're get'n low on meat. Ain't no good way to preserve how we're goin." Ada looked around and hoped that a solution would come to her.

"Not much farther and I can find more carrots and berries," Therese suggested.

"Ahmma make a bow," Ada sighed. "There jist ain't much't work with."

Every night as they ran north Ada assembled the bow bit by bit and crafted additional arrows using boughs, sinew, and skin.

"It'll work, Therese, Ah won't let us starve none." Ada did not feel as confident as she sounded. She was more of a bounty hunter, now rancher, than she ever was a survivalist.

The work took up her free time and whenever sleep escaped her in the night even when it wasn't her watch. Therese watched Ada with keep interest as she collected straight branches and work them down with her knife. Stone chips and bits of found bone were sharpened and used for arrowheads. Therese contributed when she saw an opportunity. The bone and stone chips had been Therese's contribution while Ada did the rest.

"Done, fer now, Ah guess." Ada held the completed bow up along with the meager stock of arrows and gazed at them with her brow furrowed.

"It will do Ada, we will not die." Therese asserted.

"Ah've gotta work on my aim." Ada's aim had been true with a rifle, and only a little wild with her six-shooters. She had enough experience with her Pere and bow hunting. "Ah'm a mite better with a rifle than a bow." Ada looked at the ground and kicked at a stone.

At dawn, as soon as the sun lightened the sky, Therese grabbed the arrows and bow and walked to the edge of their camp. Ada watched for movement in the distance with the pursuing campfires on her mind.

She stabbed the arrows into the ground just as the dew was drying. In a fluid and silent movement, she retrieved each arrow and with a quiet power drove each into a nearby tree.

Ada marveled at Therese's aim and skill. "Well Ah'll be damn." Ada pushed her hat back. "Ah didn't know ya could shoot."

Therese's cheeks turned a light shade of red. "I'm a quick learner," she said, cocking her eyebrow. "My older brothers showed me. I hunted rabbits on the estate."

"Estate?" Ada repeated. The furrow in her own brow deepened and her mouth turned. "Who'r ya, Therese?" she slowly asked as Therese gazed off into the distance.

All of the arrows spent, Therese turned to Ada. "I am just me," she stated and ripped an arrow from the tree. She gave Ada a small, shy smile.

That smile struck Ada.

She chuckled softly.

It was the first time in a long while Ada laughed. She couldn't hold it in; maybe it was from the prolonged tension. It felt foreign and startled her.

Therese smiled and retrieved the remaining arrows. As she bent down to grab one of the arrows, the bow fell apart. Therese was shocked.

Tilting her hat back, Ada looked up. "Well, that's that."

Therese looked at the crumbling bow in disbelief.

"Ah ain't never made nuthin like that before." Ada admitted.

Therese looked at Ada incredulously.

Winter was looming, but had not yet set in, so thankfully there was still game to be had. Traveling was slow and hard, but Ada and Therese kept ahead of the trailing campfire.

Each day they were being pushed further from their homes. Ada resented the men who hunted them and longed for the small patch of peace and quiet of her own land. Ada's sleep, ever evasive, was fraught with dreams of death.

She dreamed of the deaths of her family, the deaths of bounties, and the death in the street outside Peace's Place. After those deaths were relived, she would dream of her own death.

Awake and running, Ada could picture the nightmares where she had been stabbed, shot, hanged, drugged, and trampled. She never left the world calmly or cleanly. She would wake startled and drenched with sweat.

Therese kept a wary eye on her. "You have demons. They also hunt you."

"We jist need to keep move'n." Ada always replied.

In contrast their fears, they were in a land rich with life. Even deep in the fall with the threat of winter approaching, there was growth and possibility. They held tightly onto their meager hopes.

Ada considered backtracking and leading their pursuers astray. However, the little time they had was precious.

"If Ah could jest get 'em off our trail. . ." Ada mused. "Leadin them away from us might be worth it. Ah'd just have ta watch and make sure Ah didn't cross 'em."

Therese put her hand on Ada's arm. "No, you don't have the bullets to fight them if they catch you." Therese's eyes glistened wetly. "You cannot die now."

"Yeah, yer right. Winter's roll'n in, and Ah ain't leave'n ya." Ada gave a Therese a firm hug.

Therese let herself soften and pressed into Ada. Muscles warm and firm, Ada held onto to Therese and felt stronger for it.

"We'll make it," Ada asserted, the spark of hope ignited once again.

They had been traveling north for a week and did their best with avoiding trails and outcroppings. The gentle roll of the hills eventually gave way to steeper and rockier terrain. The trees became taller and thicker, and game surrounded them and seemed plentiful. They moved slowly and foraged often for roots and berries. Their wounds were slowly healing, although both would bear scars of their encounter at Peace's.

Occasionally, they heard the sound of horses on the wind in the distance and would hide. Ada noticed that they were getting leaner and stronger. A few times they even came across wild horses.

"Damn, what Ah wouldn't give for a bit a rope." Ada looked longingly at the stallions and mares.

"They're falling behind." Therese motioned to the bandits far behind them.

"Gettin harder on them too," Ada said. As the threat of pursuit lessened, so did their tensions.

Occasionally, Therese would hum and liven their spirits.

"What'r those songs," asked Ada one evening at dusk. As she spoke, she saw her breath and she became frightened.

"My mother," answered Therese. "She used to sing them during mass. They are the songs of Jesus," she explained. "My mother would sing them around the home and in our garden. They are in my heart," Therese closed her eyes and squeezed her hand over her chest, "with my mother."

Ada saw the glimmer of tears in Therese's eye and gave Therese's hand a gentle squeeze.

Ada noticed small flakes of snow falling. "We near?" Ada said, her voice a little higher than usual.

"Yes."

Dark clouds hung low, but the heavier snows held off; only small eddies of flakes occasionally drifted around them.

Therese and Ada continued onward, getting stiffer, and hunching over more as the elements bore down on them. The cold was growing and digging into them.

CHAPTER NINE

After two long weeks of running and starving, Ada and Therese finally arrived at their destination. They walked around a rise and came upon a wall of stacked stones. Ada was surprised to find Therese had led them to a shelter built like the one she had built with William.

Therese displayed a sweet smile of recognition as she walked slowly toward the door. They found a well-built storm wall with a sturdy door and slots to fire out of.

"This's a hold," Ada exclaimed, slapping her leg. "Ah've used 'em myself a time or two," added Ada. "These're scattered all about fer folks't use." The wall was flanked by the natural rise and Ada would've missed it had Therese not led her there directly.

Therese opened the door and both women instantly gagged as the heavy and thick scent of rot assaulted them.

Ada covered her nose and mouth as Therese lurched to the side and vomited. Quick to recover, Ada peered into the blackness before them. A cold drizzle started and wetted their shoulders as Ada threw Therese her bandana and steeled herself for what she was sure to see.

Ada looked to Therese e she finally stopped heaving.

Therese nodded silently. She had fear in her eyes and her mouth was drawn, her skin pallid. Mouths and noses covered as best they could, they entered. It took a moment for their eyes to adjust, and when they did. . .

"Dear God," Ada muttered.

Therese made the sign of the cross upon herself.

Bodies littered the floor.

"These folks been here fer a spell," Ada commented as she carefully stepped among the husk-dry corpses. "They ain't dressed like eastern folk, and Ah don't think they were on tha lamb neither. Looks like a big family; men, women, an children."

Therese looked as though she were in shock.

Ada put a consoling hand on Therese's shoulder. "They been here a while, pro'ly since last winter. Must'a been trapped or somethin." Her eyes swept the room, but Ada didn't notice any weapons. A quick survey of the shelter showed no bullet holes or casings so far as she could see. "Hope it weren't sickness," Ada muttered more to herself than to Therese.

Ada put eyes upon Therese and guided her out of the structure. Therese looked distant and distracted.

"We gotta bury 'em," Ada finally said. "Could burn 'em, but I don't want the smoke ta draw anyone."

"No, we will bury them," Therese said quickly and furtively.

Ada frowned and looked at the ground, not sure what else to say. "We got to get 'em in the ground fore the dirt seizes up from the cold." Ada looked to the sky as the cold drizzle continued.

With faces covered and wearing makeshift gloves, Ada and Therese lined up the bodies outside the structure.

"Looks like they really was traveling together," Ada said upon noting the similarities in their clothing. "Well, we know what we are working with, so let's get to it." Ada started scooping dirt with a piece of stone.

They had picked a clearing to the west of the door where the land started to roll away. Using their hands, sticks, and stones, it took two days to bury the dead. It was hard, grueling work, and neither woman spoke much. They worked together in this single purpose while putting the thoughts of their own pursuit out of mind.

They worked from before the sun was up until the sun set. When the did rest, they did it with the door open. They had carried all of the bodies outside, but still worried about the vestiges of disease. Yellow fever, cholera, and other even stranger diseases occupied their unspoken thoughts. All of the blankets and clothes were buried with the dead. They didn't leave so much as a scrap of cloth in the shelter.

At the end of the second day, Ada was wiping sweat from her brow when she noticed Therese. Silently, she watched the beautiful Mexican woman walk to each grave. Therese stopped at each site and whispered something before moving on.

Therese turned and tied up her thick black curls with Ada's bandanna and a glint of silver caught the sun. Ada tried to remember seeing the necklace on Therese and was sure she hadn't. Ada frowned at the thought of Therese taking from the bodies and walked over.

"What's that about," she asked, pointing to the necklace. "Ya sure it's safe ta wear?" Ada held Therese's gaze and continued, "These folks died in a bad way." Ada was not outwardly accusing Therese of anything, but Therese understood.

"I did not steal this," Therese said while calmly fingering the chain. "It was uncle's."

Ada stood stock still in shock. "Hold on now." Ada collected herself and, after a moment, continued, "Ya knew these folks an didn't say anything? Is this how ya knew'a this spot?" Ada was confused and angry.

Therese looked at the ground and spoke quietly, "I did not expect anyone to be here."

Ada reflected on the terrible situation they'd stumbled upon. Two days had passed while they buried the people, Therese's people.

"It don't change nothin," Ada asserted. "But damn girl," she pulled Therese into a hug.

Therese heavy sobs were muffled by Ada shirt. They stood that way under the pines until the rain stopped.

Only once the bodies were buried and many prayers had been said did the two women realize they were starving.

"Let's hunt," Ada suggested to Therese, and Therese nodded in agreement.

They followed the gentle roll of the hill to the west and came across a small creek.

"Well, we got water," Ada shrugged. She spotted deer crossing to the north and, taking turns with the bow, Ada and Therese were able to fell two deer. Both shots had been clear and true. "Damn, that's a good shot," Ada observed. Therese smiled, a small bit of pride showing in her eyes.

Time was consumed by the preparations necessary for them to survive the winter. Every day Ada saw her breath thicker in the morning air. Cool, crisp, and smoky, she blew into the sky and watched the birds overhead flying south. The cold rain turned to sleet, and eventually, the sleet became snow.

At that time, all of nature around the shelter ground to a halt. Having taken care of both food and shelter, Therese and Ada occupied their time in other ways. Using clay from the creek bed, they patched in the wall of stones and fortified the shelter, anything to keep busy.

Ada made another bow and kept her guns clean and oiled. She showed Therese how she rendered fat and they worked together dissembling and assembling the guns. They boiled water in the skulls of the animals they killed. Therese watched in amazement as Ada used everything from an animal.

"Yer people taught ya this?" Therese gawked.

"Yeah," Ada said as she shaved a bone into an arrowhead. "We was pretty poor, ah guess, didn't waste nothin." Ada sorted her few remaining bullets and sighed. "There ain't no need now, but Ah don't wanna get caught flat-footed by those fellas, not again."

The two women found that everything that they needed for food was provided by the bows and their steady hands. They hunted until the game was scarce while they kept an eye out for riders each day. Four days after the bodies had all been buried, they saw the campfire in the distance.

"Ah wonder if that's them?" Ada squinted into the darkness. As if in answer, a volley of gunfire erupted in the darkness.

"That's them," sighed Therese. She bit her lip in worry.

Winter arrived gradually. The cold and damp turned to frost and ice, the ground seized up, and the animals hid. There was little movement. Silence permeated the biting cold as snow began accumulating slowly with each day.

Ada swore and grumbled as the conditions grew harsh. Their food stores were ample and their shelter secured. Inside the den they had kept two bows and stack of arrows after cleaning them as best they could and praying to purify them of any disease. The bows and arrows were well made.

"These'll do," Ada said. She threw one to Therese and she caught it deftly.

"As long as you did not make them," replied Therese bitterly.

Therese built a small ingle and lit a fire near a wall. The smoke escaped through the rifle slots.

"We're dug in now." Ada did not like winter. "Damn snow'll slow us down."

"It will slow them too as well as hide us," Therese added.

Ada nodded and thought back on how close she had come to the Preacher. "Out'o the frying pan and inta tha fire," she said to herself.

Therese cocked an eyebrow, but said nothing.

Snow fell in great amounts until everything was buried under the soft white powder. The landscape was a contrast of pure white snow and deep black tree trunks.

Ada and Therese watched a storm head bear down from the north.

"That's gonna be a bad one," Ada pointed out.

Therese nodded and had a worried look in her eye. "I have not been in a winter like this," she said. "We never went this far north when I was young."

Ada gave a gentle whistle. "Ah try an avoid 'em myself; don't care much for winter, and sure as hell don't care fer snow. Yer in for somethin big Ah reckon," Ada added while looking to the sky.

When the clouds finally cracked open, they released a wild flurry. The wind was high and drove the snow with ferocity.

"Ain't no riders come'n out this way." Ada peered through the single rifle slot above the inglenook. The north wind stung her eyes. "Rider couldn't see their horse's ears in this." Ada doubted their pursuers were searching for them in this weather. Ada thought back to a storm she'd experienced while in Arkansas. "Been in a bad one like this before," she told Therese as Therese huddled herself into a warm corner.

"Ah climbed and climbed, walked so many damn steps that day." Ada told Therese how she had found herself on a tower at Hot Springs. "There was this old codger charg'n folks ta see from tha top. Mind you, it was high and a mighty fine view." Ada leaned her back against the wall and tilted her hat back as she reminisced. "Close to God as Ah ever been," she whispered. "Ah looked all round and lost my breath; ain't nuthin like bein up there."

Therese watched Ada closely as Ada's gaze focused themselves on the past.

"Ah caught buzzards soarin' at eye level, and all tha roads were thin like fence wire." Ada paused before continuing slowly, "Horses looked to be like wooden toys. Ah'd forgot to breath," she chuckled a bit and gave Therese a sheepish smirk. "A storm, like this," Ada tilted her head to the wall, "was comin down from the north. Saw this heavy wall of darkness even if it was still a ways off."

Ada recalled the vast enormity of what she had seen, savoring the memory before continuing, "When the sun went down, Ah got misty-eyed," her voice cracked.

"You were changed," added Therese. "God can do that, God is in your heart."

Stirred, Ada replied, "At church, Ah never felt like that. The sermons were all about anger and suffer'n."

"God is not just in the sermons," Therese pointed out. "God is in you, in the water, the land, and the goodness in people."

Ada turned this over, "Ah'd a liked yer sermons a mite better."

Therese's face flushed and she turned her head.

Ada scuffed her shoe's toe against the ground. "Was there fer a bounty, Ah couldn't sleep, and nuthin felt right. Tha storm broke that night, and the wind ripped at everythin; people scurried like mice and hunkered down. Tha snow piled up fierce; it smothered everythin and left scars on the town as well as the people." Ada shrugged and let a moment of silence pass. "Ah drank in a bar in town that night. Jest sat quietly and thought. 'Eventually, tha fella Ah was after came in and got stove on rye. He drank hisself right off the stool."

Therese chuckled.

"Walked over to him, slow and heavy. Told him Ah was collectin him, but Ah don't think he knew what was happenin." She added, "Too drunk. Couldn't leave though, the snow was still blowin hard and pilin up." Ada's face turned sour. "Just drank with him for a few days. He was a shyster, bilked a widow outta her inheritance. Weren't nuthin 'bout him, 'cept he thought was smart'n everybody else. We was there two weeks jist drink'n and wait'n." Ada sighed and sat down with her back to the wall. She chewed on a piece of leather she carried.

Therese watched quietly and waited. The wind howled outside and whistled through the gaps in the walls.

"'Ventually, it stopped." Ada shrugged. "Left Hot Springs together, he, hogtied and on the ass end of his horse. We had ta tread careful and it took us a bit to get back." Ada paused, talking slowly, "Ah led us back to Jackson and collected on him."

She thought and said nothing for a few moments.

"Nothin looked tha same after that day," Ada continued. "Tha fire in my belly was low, and Ah didn't know where Ah stood on anythin." Ada pulled off her boots and rubbed her feet. Her hands went to her shirt and she undid the top buttons. "Ah knew that if Ah didn't git up and go, Ah'd never get after that Preacher." She sighed and looked at the ceiling.

Therese nodded and said, "You will get him Ada, I am sure of it."

Ada nodded and closed her eyes as a single tear fell into the darkness.

Therese slept by the smoldering coals. Ada turned and looked at her in the night. Therese was small and dark where Ada was broad and had lighter hair. They were two sides of a coin. Ada appreciated Therese being with her even though she held guilt for getting Therese involved.

The Mexican woman slept deep and seemed comfortable. As they did on the lamb, they took turns on the lookout. They continued mostly out of habit, but also to watch for a break in the storm. The door was almost snowed in, and they had to continually clear it out.

"We ain't gett'n buried in here," said Ada.

Therese nodded, worrying her lip. "What of William," asked Therese.

"What of him," Ada responded sharply.

The wind howled through the gun slot. There was little warmth in the small moving flames that occasionally shot up from the coals.

Ada looked deeply into the small flames. "He's a friend," she finally said, "Sorry fer be'in short with ya."

"It is nothing," Therese answered as she cast a sidelong glance at Ada. Therese mustered up her courage and asked, "Are you two. . . ?"

Ada smiled ruefully, "Think he wants ta be, but it's not fer me." Her mind went to the Preacher. "He's good though. Through and through, honest, and loyal, he is."

Therese nodded and looked at the flames. "He is good to my little brother." Therese bit her lip and fingered her necklace's chain, "I hope he's safe."

"Ah'm sure he is; that town'll look out for him."

As the tension of being hunted faded, they were left with their worries of being buried alive and freezing to death.

"Ya think this is what happened ta yer people," asked Ada.

Therese shrugged. "Maybe. They didn't fight and they didn't look sick." Therese considered Ada's question further and continued, "They might've been trapped in here last winter." She fingered her necklace.

Furtive glances to each other confirmed the reminder of Ada and Therese's own desperate situation. The wind and snow continued beating against the shelter.

One night, as Therese drifted to sleep, she saw Ada praying. She said nothing, but her worry increased.

Chapter Ten

A few more days passed before eventually the storm broke and Ada and Therese woke to a pervasive silence. They peered out the rifle slots and found that the weather had indeed buried them alive.

"We'll get outta this." Ada put her hand on Therese's arm and gave her a gentle squeeze.

Therese offered a half-smile and a nod.

It took fire, boiled water, and a makeshift shovel to carve their way out of their shelter as both women worked together to push their way out.

"Whatever in the world happened to yer folk," Ada asked while looking at the snow where the graves would be and rubbed her neck.

Therese chewed her lip and frowned. "I don't know; they were trapped by something." No new answers came.

"Must've been something fierce," Ada said.

Therese nodded and looked away.

The better part of a day passed before they could both easily get out.

"Finally out," Ada gave her knee a slap, "hot smack a rabbit," she hollered with relief.

Therese's stomach growled audibly.

"Time to hunt, then," observed Ada.

Therese smiled and rolled her eyes.

In the blinding light of day, they separated, each on the hunt. They nodded to each other and set out in opposite directions. Each stepped through the deep snow, lively and alert, eventually finding themselves far from the shelter.

Almost immediately, Therese found tracks and signs of life. Blue skies teased out life from the earth, and the animals emerged from burrow and nest to a world blanketed in white. The game Therese found was small. She brought down a few birds and a single white rabbit. While Therese had success with the bow, Ada had her sights set on their pursuers.

Ada, however, found nothing. There were no human tracks or horse tracks to be seen. Everything had been buried by the snow. She was relieved to have apparently lost the Mexicans and was ready to return home. Ada was making her way back to Therese when a tree near her exploded in a shower of frozen sap and wood splinters. The rapport of a rifle followed.

Ada threw herself to the ground. Warm blood darkened the pristine snow. Ada touched her forehead where a piece of wood had slicked a gash into her skin. "Damn, yer either a crack shot, or lucky as fuck," Ada cursed.

Ada rolled behind a tree while staying close to the ground. Someone had been watching and waiting. After securing herself behind the tree, Ada unshouldered her rifle. She propped herself on one knee and peered through the scope in search of her quarry.

"Where are ya, ya sonofabitch?" Ada hissed through her teeth.

There were two dark silhouettes atop a hill across a valley of peerless snow from Ada. Ada, meanwhile, was in a thick clump of trees that left her sheltered and out of sight. She saw the glint of light reflected by the scope lens of the man who'd shot her.

"Ya jist gave me a target ta aim fer, ya damn ass." She breathed out and slowly pulled the trigger.

One of the man-shaped shadows jerked and slumped. The second dark shape turned and ran back down the hill and out of Ada's line of sight.

"God damn it," Ada swore and stood. The plodding of horses was carried to her ears by the wind.

Ada looped her rifle over her shoulder and ran toward the sound while drawing a pistol as she crossed the lowland. Ada ran up the slope and crested the ridge, but found no one.

"Shit, he gone." Ada spun around and took in the landscape. "Must'a woven into tha trees," she angrily muttered to herself before catching sight of some wooded cover.

That was when she noticed the hobbled horse. A gentle smile played across Ada's lips that almost touched her eyes. "Hey there girl," Ada spoke softly and held her hands open.

In the snow beside the horse was a limp, dark figure marring the otherwise white landscape.

Ada turned him over with her foot. He appeared to be one of the men that had been trailing her and Therese. He was dark-skinned and had black hair. There was nothing on him that identified him.

"Well, yer one of 'em," Ada said as she set eyes upon his stirrups. "Ya was there in tha street," she said as she sat back on her heels and rifled through his pockets.

The horse gave a soft chuff behind Ada.

"Come along girl," Ada walked carefully back to the horse. She softly patted the horse's neck and took hold of the reins.

Ada let the dark red quarter horse nose around her and her clothes. She gave Ada no trouble as put the dead man across her haunches. Ada looked around for the rifle and scope she had heard and seen; however, it was gone, probably taken off into the woods by the other figure. She did find ammunition on the dead man, which was a help. However, it was the packet of coffee and a tin cup that excited Ada the most.

Ada took her time with the quarter horse as she tethered her to a nearby tree. Ada removed the hobble rope and the horse stamped in the snow.

"It'll be alright girl, that nasty man ain't gonna do nuthin to ya." Ada patted the quarter horse. "Ya a good things, ain't ya. We got carrots Therese found ya'll like." She thought about riding the horse back to the shelter, but led her instead. "Don't need ta rush things, we'll get along fine soon 'nough."

The horse gave Ada no resistance as she was led to the shelter.

Therese gasped with surprise upon sighting them. "What is this?"

"A horse," Ada replied wryly.

"I know that just looking. But where did it come from?" Therese pressed.

"One of them fellas that shot up Peace's gave it ta me."

Therese was pale and trembled. "Please do not joke Ada," she said with tears in her eyes. "Who was the man?"

"Not Alejandro," Ada said. "It was one of tha other fellas."

She recounted to Therese the encounter in the woods.

Therese looked at the dead man closely once she was sure it was not Alejandro. "Even in death, evil has power." Therese shook her head. She did not know the man.

The two women stripped him of what remained of his gear and brought the shying quarter horse into the shelter.

"Well, she'll fit here fer now. Wasn't sure bout the door, but worked aright," Ada said.

Therese nodded. "They will come."

"'Bout time to get this over with, huh?"

Therese nodded. "I will run no more," she stated with finality.

Therese fed the small and dark quarter horse wild carrots and brushed her with the Mexican's tack. In the saddle bags, they had discovered an assortment of supplies and even a length of rope.

Ada puzzled over what to do with the body. "Ah don't wanna put him with good folk," Ada said as she dug her toe into the ground.

"We can throw him the creek," suggested Therese.

"Nah, that'll spoil the water down a ways. Ah'd leave 'em to wolves, but that'd just draw 'em here." She looked at the ceiling. "There's rocks, down by the crik," Ada considered. "Can use them."

Therese agreed.

Therese and Ada brought the corpse down the rolling hill from their shelter and into a rocky outcropping where they buried the man under a pile of stones. The had to scrape snow away from the rocks and spent the long day in labor. The activity cleared Ada's head.

"Your hands are so strong," Therese observed as they finished covering the man.

Ada colored lightly. "Been working with 'em my entire life. They do aright." Ada looked at her calluses and thick knuckles. "My fists got hard and wits got sharp," Ada added. Ada shook her head and turned to Therese. "They know where we are, so we gotta be ready."

Therese nodded and chewed on her lip.

Ada used the rope from the dead man's belongings to hitch the horse to a tree during the day when the quarter horse would scrape up grass from under the snow.

"Now we are feeding three mouths," observed Therese, "and winter is not over."

Ada shrugged. "She'll be alright, jist gotta move'er around to fresh spots. It's how the wild ones do it."

Ada and Therese took turns foraging for wild carrots and dry grasses. Food for the horse was hard to come by and took extra time. Fortunately, they had stock-piled meat and the saddle bags contained some hardtack.

Therese's prayers at night were for the two of them.

Ada watched, gratefully, in silence. "We need all tha help we can get," Ada said as she put her hand upon Therese's shoulder.

Therese's small and gentle hand went to Ada's. There was a stillness and warmth that they shared, one that required no words.

The winter days dragged along, and waiting to get ambushed made them feel even longer. It was quiet in the woods, and Ada and Therese found comfort in each other and the simple duty of caring for the horse.

Ada quickly fell into her old rituals. She brushed the dark red quarter horse's thick and rich winter coat daily. After the horse was brushed down, she picked her hooves. The entire time Ada spoke gently to her using small utterances and gentle phrases. Sometimes she spoke about the present, less frequently she mentioned the past. In this way, Therese learned about the Preacher.

"Ah trust you, Therese," Ada said one day. "That doesn't happen offen, but Ah know ya got my back."

"Yes, I do, you can count on me, always."

"We ride together, that means somethin' to me," Ada added looking from Therese's eyes to the land around her.

"I do not know what that man did to you, but I am sorry he caused you pain," Therese spoke with compassion.

Ada's face tightened along with the rest of the muscles in her body. "Yeah, Ah gotta end 'im. He killt folks close ta me," Ada told Therese more of her story than what she'd overheard.

Tears streamed down Therese's small face. She held Ada close as she tried to take the sadness and pain from her.

Ada softened in Therese's arms. Their breathing became as one and they held each other through the night.

During this time, all three grew lean, but managed to stay healthy. There were no more storms, and they scouted for their pursuers daily. Sometimes they saw small campfires at night that were far off. Neither Ada nor Therese could be sure who lit the fires; they only knew that caution was their only option.

"They gettin closer and try'n to keep hid," Ada realized. "They got our scent, jist can't make sense'o where we are."

Therese smiled and patted the wall of the shelter. "Either that, or they smell this here horse." Therese looked out the door at the growing pile of manure.

"Yeah, she's a handful, ain't she," Ada sighed and was purposefully vague.

Therese shook her head.

They took to calling the shelter Armond's, after Therese's uncle. The place was not his, as it belonged to nobody. It was a way station, a spot for travelers and the hunted to hunker down. Each visitor had been there for a different purpose over the years; some had been chased there like Ada and Therese, while others had merely been crossing the land and needed a place to wait out the weather. Some had run there to hide or escape with a loved one while seeking greener pastures. As the snow began to melt and the danger they were in increased, Therese told Ada her own story.

Ada had stoked embers until they made small licking flames. Therese and Ada had brushed the horse together. Boots off, Ada nursed a cup of coffee she had taken from the bandit.

Therese sat with her back to the wall and stared into the flickering flames. "My name is Therese Marie Martinez," she started.

Ada looked at Therese over the cup and sat still, intent on hearing everything.

"I was born in a Catholic household to two strong parents. My people came from a town just north of Mexico City. My father," she choked back a sob.

Ada stood and walked over to Therese. She sat beside her friend and put her arm around her.

"He and his brother worked the land together, and my mother ran our corner store where she sold the crops my father and uncle grew. She was humble, quiet, and hard-working," Therese said quietly.

"Like you," Ada said while gently giving Therese a small squeeze and a soft smile. "They were people who loved animals and measured the quality of the land with their fingers."

"My family were sharecroppers. They worked the land as tenants to a very wealthy man," Therese continued. "Even though they were very capable, nature often worked against them." Therese started to speak faster, "There were three bad seasons for their crops, and demands from the landlord could not be met. My mother, Elsa, started sending my brothers and sisters to work in the wealthy man's home."

Therese paused and, for a time, both women watched the flames ebb and flow as Therese worked up the strength to continue.

"I worked in the fields," Therese said. "Everything went like this for a long time, then I became a woman," Therese gave a shudder and Ada cringed. "There was a man in the house. He was one of the hired guns, the fastest and most acclaimed," Therese's knuckles were white and shook like fresh laundered sheets in the wind. "He took an interest in me."

"He made advances," she spat, "and tried to court me. But I resisted. Often, he was not around.   Most of the time he was sent out to kill or pressure someone. He made the half-man very much money."

Ada's eyebrow went up. "Half-man? What the hell was the other half?"

Therese relaxed and chuckled. "He was hurt in the war. His wife would yell that he was 'half a man,' I know no more."

It was Ada's turn to chuckle. "Put'n two and two together," she said with a nod.

Therese continued, "With Alejandro, there was little that stirred him and even less he cared about. He was smug and cruel," Therese shook with each word. "Alejandro stayed in the big home, as he was favored for his duties. People feared Alejandro because he was a soldier for evil." Therese put the sign of the cross upon herself. "Fierce and quick, he was sure of himself in all things," Therese paused and caught her breath.

Ada held her tightly.

"I ignored and refused his advances. He was shocked," Therese said as she looked over and into Ada's eyes.

"Ya can stop," offered Ada.

Therese shook her head. "I need it out."

Therese eventually stopped shaking and relaxed in Ada's arms.

She continued without the previous tones of fear, "He stalked me around the house and watched me at dinner. I cooked the meals and the rich man and his wife loved everything that I made."

"Ah was wondering who had been make'n my breakfasts at Peace's. Was sure it wasn't Ms. Peace." She threw a shrewd look upon Therese who blushed a deep and vibrant crimson. Eventually Therese continued with her tale. "Alejandro asked the rich man for my hand, and he gave it as if it was his," a fire burned in Therese's eyes as she spoke. "I ran to my mother, but she was afraid for me. She was like a statue, her eyes filled with tears as she told me to be strong." Therese bent over beside the bed of coals and circled her arms around her knees. "My mother was a calm woman, but she had a storm inside her. That night, a blaze broke out in the bedroom, and the boss and his wife were burned." Therese adjusted her legs before continuing, "They did not escape in their opium-induced stupor. And I ran. Alejandro cursed me and blamed me for the loss of his money and power." Therese shuddered, "now he hunts me for his pound of flesh."

Ada spat into the fire. "Ah'll be damned if he gits anythin."

Therese dreamed that night of charred and scorched earth. She dreamed of being chased by faceless bandits, and, in her dreams, she ran and dodged while staying just feet ahead of her pursuers.

Ada observed Therese's fitful sleep. She rested a hand upon the smaller woman, occasionally offering soothing words. Ada already wanted Alejandro's blood for firing at her, shooting up Peace's, and for running her off her land. Now, she wanted to protect Therese.

"In a fair fight, Ah would'a taken 'im," she said. "Next time, Ah'll do it."

CHAPTER ELEVEN

The day Ada and Therese both dreaded and prepared for finally arrived.

Ada was fashioning fresh arrowheads from shards of stone and tossing them to Therese. "We'll git him," she said quietly.

Therese nodded and a tear slid down her cheek.

"Ya smell that?" Ada asked. She glanced at the small inglenook, but it was stone cold.

"Smoke," observed Therese.

The horse nickered and turned its ears up.

Ada patted her neck and cooed, "it's alright girl." She put the saddle on the quarter horse and cinched the girth with a snap.

The horse chomped at her bit, ready and raring to move as Ada and Therese armed themselves.

"Move slow'n low," Ada said.

Therese nodded and followed.

"They on top'o us." Ada tossed a glance to the earth above the shelter.

"There's the smoke," Therese aid upon spotting the bandit camp.

"It's them, Ah hear Spanish," Ada observed.

Therese nodded.

The women moved to cover far enough away from the shelter in order to see what lay on top of the rise.

"They got a few horses," Ada counted.

"And quite a few men," Therese finished.

"Ya ready fer this," asked Ada.

"I will run no more," stated Therese.

Ada tilted her head in agreement. "Let's see what they do fore we rush'em."

The sun, rolling along the horizon, set without fanfare. The men, both bored and angry at the cold, began drinking and cursing in anger under their breath as a means to stay warm. Snow remained on the ground, but receded from the heat of their low and shrouded campfire where it became mud under their feet. Both the men's and horses' breaths were visible in the cold night.

One of the men's number wandered toward the edge of the hill to relieve himself. The ground was hard and slick at the edge, and he slid and fell into the darkness. He tumbled down the back of the hill and eventually landed hard on the ground, where he remained in a groggy and dazed state. All he could see were the faint outlines of trees and a few glimmers of firelight upon the snow. Eventually he stood and, turning around, spotted the door of Ada and Therese's shelter.

For a moment, he pondered the door. Eventually he realized what it was: He'd found that woman they were hunting.

The man's smile split his hairy face and he threw his arm into the air. Just as he was calling out to the others of his posse, Ada's knife slit his throat. The gash was jagged and deep. Blood poured from the man's torn neck as his eyes flashed and glazed over.

Ada eased the shaking body to the ground and quickly patted him down in search of weapons. A pool of dark blood sunk into the white snow.

"Alejandro is near," Therese said while throwing Ada a furtive glance. Therese had donned one of Ada's gun belts and a bandoleer. Her expression was fierce as it flashed between desperate rage and all-consuming fear.

Ada's face tightened in worry. She signaled Therese to be ready.

Therese grabbed the horse's lead as Ada circled around and made her way up the hill.

The startled men, roused by the shout, ran toward the ridge. They pointed and yelled upon seeing a woman riding out on one of their horses.

Safely in the trees, Therese pulled at the reigns and turned. "Alejandro," she yelled, "come and die tonight."

"Who—" Alejandro pushed passed his men. He peered into the darkness and saw the faint outlines of a familiar woman.

It was the girl who had ruined his life.

Alejandro's bellows of rage followed her into the forest.

The men braced themselves to fire into the forest as Ada made her way up the rise. She was enraged by these men who had hunted her and had fired on Ms. Peace and her place. The Preacher was not in the group, but she used her anger at him to push her past reason. Fueled with a white hot and searing blaze of righteous anger, she ran over the hill and yelled, "Die ya bastards!" She lifted both pistols and blasted fire upon the men.

Blood spurted from wounds made by the fire of Ada's six-shooters. Ada, roaring like an animal, fired into gut, limb, and head with reckless abandon. "Ah'm gonna kill all ya'll sonsobitches!" Ada screamed over the rapport of the guns.

Men missing their kneecaps fell into the snow. The man next to Alejandro fell backward off the ridge while clutching a hole in his chest as blood poured through his fingers.

Alejandro spun away from Ada and leapt behind a small collection of crates and supplies.

A man across the fire from Ada drew his gun and shot into the ground as Ada shot his jaw clean off. Shock flew across his eyes as he clutched the roof of his mouth and ran into the darkness before falling dead into the snow from another bullet.

Ada was firing at close range, and most of the shots she fired found a mark.

Once the six-shooters were emptied of their bullets, Ada threw her pistols to the ground and dropped to one knee. A bullet nicked her hat and tossed it into the snow.

"Damn," she cursed as she slid the rifle off her shoulder and fired quickly through the assembled posse—what was left standing of it, anyway.

Meanwhile, Therese had ridden to an adjacent hill and was firing a volley of arrows back at her pursuers. One by one bleeding men perforated with arrows and bullet holes dropped to the snow until the snow-covered hill was black with blood.

Alejandro rolled away from the firelight and into the shadows. He pulled a corpse toward himself and lay still. His breathing came ragged and fast as he slowly drew a large and wicked blade. He had spent his bullets firing at Therese as she rode through the trees, leaving him with only this. "I will kill both of you witches," he swore under his breath. He tensed, muscles ready to pounce.

Alejandro noticed Ada weaving toward him, then past him, through the field littered with his fallen—some bleeding and moaning, others dead—men. He could hear—and feel—Therese and her horse's thundering hooves drawing near.

"Where ya at señor," Ada yelled. "Ah know yer 'round here somewhere."

Suddenly, a hand thrust out of a pile of bodies and dragged Ada to the earth, knocking the wind out of her.

Thrown off balance, Ada dropped her rifle.

A man covered with gore grappled with her. His thick hand grabbed her throat and his other hand formed a fist.

Punch after punch struck Ada until her eye was swollen and her organs in her gut bruised.

He struck again and again, raising his hand high into the air before pummeling her with hatred in his eyes.

As he pulled back for another hit, Ada lifted her hips and turned, throwing Alejandro to the side.

He staggered onto one knee and stabbed at her side with the long knife.

She gasped and grunted as the blade sliced through her flesh. Bright lights popped in her head as her clothes became warm and sticky with her own blood. Ada found herself on her knees and readied herself for whatever blow Alejandro was going to carry out next.

He growled like a beast and turned to fully stand as he dragged out his blade. He smiled with a small, crooked grin—

Suddenly, an arrow hit him in his shoulder. The next second, another arrow pierced his leg. Another then struck his side.

Alejandro backed away as Therese barreled up the hill and screamed. Their eyes met and he howled.

Therese leapt off the horse and ran at Alejandro with an arrow in her hand, now too close to use the bow.

Alejandro swung his knife wide and Therese slid under the wide arch of the blade.

Therese rose beside him and kicked at Alejandro's knee.

Alejandro's leg buckled and he struck the ground hard.

Therese spun and stabbed the arrow into Alejandro's neck before ripping it back out.

Thick and viscous blood ran over her small hand, covering her in gore.

Alejandro turned and Therese thrust the arrow into his eye and all the way to the back of his skull.

Alejandro fell to the ground with a thump and lay still.

Therese stood, panting, before she fell to the ground.

The sun awoke to a blood-soaked battlefield. No songbirds greeted the day, the only sounds that of the slow and heavy step of hooves. The faded remains of the campfire gave up a small curling wisp of gray.

Ada woke to the coppery taste of blood. "What. . . where?" Ada spat blood and blinked at the soreness pervading her body. She held her hand to her ear and found that it was ringing. All she could smell was gunpowder. Every bit of her was hurt and tender.

With great care, she lifted herself from the ground. Ada's movements were slow and methodical as she adjusted herself one inch at a time until she was fully on her feet.

A sea of death spread before her. On all sides of her were the bodies of the men that had hunted herself and Therese.

Saddled horses scraped for grass nearby. The sky was still gray with winter clouds and the air frigid.

Touching the wound from the knife made her wince. Sometime during the night, she had stopped bleeding; however just standing up she tore herself open anew and blood flowed fresh from her.

Ada ripped up a bit of material from a dead man's shirt and wrapped herself with it. "You ain't gonna need it."

It took Ada a few minutes to find her guns. Her six-shooters returned to their holsters, but without any remaining ammunition. Ada used her rifle like a cane to hold herself up.

She found Alejandro dead where he lay. He'd been pierced with the arrows Ada and Therese had made together, and was riddled with bullet wounds. He had died a bloody mess.

Ada scanned the hilltop until she found the small Mexican woman lying alone.

She was still.

Ada ran to Therese's side and was startled by the feeling of Therese's cold hands. One of the men, maybe Alejandro himself, had gotten a lucky shot on Therese.

"No, no, no, no," Ada yelled desperately. Tears rolled from her cheeks into the snow and onto Therese. "Not you too," Ada cried through blood, spittle, and tears. "Damn you all, damn you all to hell," she yelled. She rocked back and forth while gently holding Therese's head in her lap. Eventually, Ada noticed the peaceful look on Therese's face. However, it only fed her rage and sadness.

Ada gently placed Therese's head back onto the snow before staggering away. She retched and heaved beside a tree nearby as the buzzards began to circle overhead.

Once she had nothing left to retch up, Ada walked over the Therese and knelt by her. She took Therese's hand and said a few prayers. Using rope, a horse, and some wood, Ada brought Therese's body back to the shelter. Once inside, she pulled at rocks on the wall and collected a small pile.

Ada then went back to the posse's camp and found a small axe. She used it to cut down a narrow pine. She tied one end the rope to the log and the other to one of the horses before wedging it into the lowest part of the doorway.

"Alright girl, let's go." Ada patted the quarter horse's neck and gave it a gentle kick with her heels. Tears cut through the dirt and blood on Ada's face as the horse pulled the rope and brought down their shelter. She tethered the horse to a tree and once the dust settled. Ada put her hands together and prayed outside Therese's makeshift tomb. As she said a final word for her friend so that she might find peace in the afterlife, Ada blacked out and fell face-first into the snow.

Ada slowly opened her eyes and was met with the dim light of dawn. A gentle breeze blew and she heard the evergreens' whisper. The snow had melted underneath her and water had soaked into her clothes.

She tensed her muscles and her mind reeled in the ensuing pain. "Where am Ah," Ada croaked.

The first thing Ada was aware of was that she had not bled to death. She saw the quarter horse nearby. The little red horse had come untethered.

"Ya still 'round girl?" Ada gave a small, ginger smile, and a sharp pain struck across her face. Tenderly and slowly she stood. There was a stabbing pain searing her side. "Ah ain't dead… so must'a missed ma organs," Ada said slowly to the horse. There was thick and caked blood drying on her clothes. "Damn, Ah'm a sight."

Ada debated whether to pull the clothes free or leave them. They might be holding back the flow of blood she reasoned.

"Ah'll leave well enough alone," she decided.

Using her rifle once again as a cane, Ada hobbled over to some branches intent on cutting one for a splint.

As the day unfolded and brought with it fresh birdsong, Ada kept to the top of the hill. Using strips of clothing and wood, she fashioned the blood-soaked brace that would hold her together.

Time slowed as Ada worked. Everything she found was weighed down by the dead. Rigging bags, she filled with hard tack, bullets, and what other useful items she could scrounge before leading the small horse from man to man and then from horse to horse, she collected supplies. There was ammunition on the bodies and she collected all she found until she'd reloaded her guns and filled both her belts and bandoleers. Even on a horse, she was days away from town.

"Ain't no tellin what trouble we'll cross, girl," Ada said as she walked the horse up to the crates.

"Those folk were poor," she noted as she took final stock of what she found. Most of what the men had was meager and in disrepair.

Only Alejandro carried anything of actual value. Ada found a fine leather holster and sawed-off shotgun. Ada belted the gun on gingerly and scrounged for any remaining shells.

"Got a few pesos too, looks like," Ada said as she patted down his thick coat. She did find a compass and, a few feet away, the bowie knife. She held it and thought of how it felt slicing through her body. It caught the sun well and was evenly balanced. "This'll do," she said as she pocketed both the compass and the knife. Everything else seemed tainted to her, or cursed.

The buzzards in the sky had grown in number. Ada needed to move soon. The wolves would be coming next.

"Come on girl, we goin back ta town," Ada said as she led the horse to a swale. Ada painstakingly mounted, cursing in pain as she stepped up into the saddle. She had to give the horse her head and Ada used her rope to tie herself to the saddle's horn. Stepping up had made her almost pass out. In this way, they rode.

The horse was headed in the direction of the town, back south and to the east. Her nose was leading her to water. Therese and Ada had crossed at least two bodies of running water during their flight.

The snow was beginning to melt in patches and grass arose from its slumber. The horse was having an easier time of it than Ada. Blood ran down Ada's thigh and she was swaying in the saddle, the ropes the only thing keeping her astride the horse.

At a creek where the quarter horse stopped to drink, Ada fell. She landed in the cold wet sand and lay still, barely breathing, passed out.

Her dreams were filled with blood and death as Ada had endless nightmares of her family. Joel and Mary looked worried, and Arden was nowhere to be found.

Ada thought she lost him and was afraid.

Mary told her to find him, Joel told her to find him. Ada screamed as the mud sucked at her boots and held her in place and she started to sink. She knew that Arden was dead , and when she looked down at the mud she saw that it was wet and oozing ichor.

Her parents, with tears running down their faces, faded away.

Ada had seen these apparitions before. Whenever she had hunted bounties, they visited her and pleaded with her. Ada had failed them, she had failed them all. The guilt consumed her.

She was trapped, helpless, and frozen. Only hatred and rage toward the Preacher kept her going.

The Preacher's shadow played across her mind and stirred her to wakefulness. Her mind filled with an all-consuming revenge and to the bloody Preacher. Her family was gone, dead. Only Ada remained. Only she could carry out the will of the dead.

The visions of her family pleaded with her to end him and bring them justice. The nightmares kept the Preacher on her mind. Her greatest fear was that he might come across her in this state.

The sand was cold on Ada's cheek. Slowly, she blinked.

Water flowed serenely ahead of her in the dim light.

Ada turned gently and propped herself on an elbow. "Damn, girl. Where we at," she muttered to the horse.

The dark red quarter horse stood ten feet away and was scraping at grass. She chuffed to Ada.

"Well," Ada mumbled as she stood. "That's mite embrass'n."

She looked for the rope and found it dangling from the saddle. The world spun around Ada as she lurched and held onto a small, hardy tree growing in the sandy mix. Whenever she moved, Ada's side erupted in pain. Placing a hand to her side, she felt the wet shirt soaked through and grimaced.

"If Ah don't do somethin' 'bout this quick. . ." she trailed off. "Ain't no time ta let this get better on its own."

She crawled into a shallow dugout the creek had made. Previous floods had exposed roots and carved out an overhang. Here she made a small fire using the dried roots she could reach.

Grunts and curses emanated from the hollow as she lifted her shirt off the wound. She saw stars in her vision and almost blacked out again as the world turned around her. A few moments passed and eventually the stars waned. Ada looked at the wound.

"Cuts clean, ya ol' dog." She did not see any pus or infection. Just to be sure, she poured some whiskey she had taken from one of the men over the wound. "Sonofabitch," she cursed while bracing herself. She cut open a shell and poured gunpowder on the gash.

As Ada cleaned and prepared the wound, she thought of Therese and her brother. She thought of Ms. Peace and of her parents.

Ada bit down on a piece of leather. She grabbed a stick from the small fire and lit the loose scattered powder. There was a loud hiss and a bright light followed by the smell of burned meat. Ada winced in pain. She lost consciousness for the third time in two days, but was no longer bleeding.

Ada and Therese had covered a great deal of ground during the ensuing run away from town on foot. The horse, even traveling slowly, still made better time.

They wove through passes and crossed several small waterways. Pockets of snow still covered the ground. In some low spots it was thicker than others.

Ada saw bear tracks and did her best to avoid the hungry animals. In the distance, she heard wolves. The red horse pinned her ears, but held her course. In the early dawn, they saw deer and turkey. Ada licked her lips and was both hungry and desperate. She chewed the hardtack she had found on the men, her other supplies already spent. The hardtack was not good, but it sustained her.

The horse pulled up any dry grass that was uncovered, or any grass she uncovered for herself. Ada's eyes were vacant and she rode without passion. The north wind whipped through them and pushed them on. She held the reins loose in her hands, merely keeping the horse's nose pointed in the right general direction and never put her heels to the horse.

They rode at a steady pace, meandering and taking longer than anyone ever would need to. Ada, heartbroken, tried to think on William, but he was too far away. She could not see him in her mind. All she saw was Therese sitting by the hearth. All she felt was her warmth and her kindness.

Therese was buried with the necklace and whatever hope Ada had left. As Ada rode, Therese's presence faded.

"Ah'm tired girl, damn tired." Ada rubbed the horse by her ears and ran her fingers through the creature's black mane. Blood-soaked and starved, she looked to the horizon and perceived nothing, not even the small town coming slowly into view. They rode in slowly before the sun. Nobody was out to see her arrive.

She rode the quarter horse along the back of the false-faced shops. Ada wanted to avoid the Preacher if he was in the town; she was afraid she would fail her family again. She thought to keep riding on in hopelessness, but stopped behind the Peace place.

Time passed and the sun rose, but Ada didn't move to go in. She sat low in the saddle and stared at the wooden wall and door facing her.

The defeat that weighed upon her now stretched back all those years ago to Louisiana. Every failure and loss added to her sadness and misery.

"Where would Ah ride," she thought. "Only death follows me."

"Maybe Ah'm cursed," Ada whispered. She felt for her gun. It was tied down and without bullets. "Ah could make it all go away," she said quietly while staring into nothingness. Ada's eyes slowly looked back to the rear door where Ms. Peace standing with her mouth open holding a bucket.

Ms. Peace ran to a confused Ada, forgetting the pail. Ada slid from the saddle into Ms. Peace's arms and let herself be held. Ms. Peace shook with muffled cries as Ada's silent tears streaked her face and soaked Ms. Peace's blouse. Ms. Peace felt the blood before she saw it and pulled away.

"Oh my God," Ms. Peace looked at her bloody hand and her eyes went wide.

Ada winced and swayed on her feet. "Good ta see ya too, Peace," she said with a wry smile playing across her lips.

"I'm here girl, come on," Ms. Peace said as she led Ada into the boarding house. Ms. Peace shot a quick glance behind them as though looking for someone.

Ada noticed and bit her lip as her vision faded to black.

Ms. Peace settled Ada into a small room behind the kitchen. "There isn't much here, but this here cot, but it'll do." Ms. Peace fussed over Ada and undressed her while talking nonstop. "A small comfort for an exhausted cook is what this is," Ms. Peace said while indicating the room.

Ada nodded, but couldn't take anything in.

She felt safe here in this place that smelled like a home. And so, Ada drifted off to sleep.

Meanwhile, Ms. Peace fetched the town doctor straightaway.

"You won't say a word of this, you have to promise," she told the doctor. "I will pay you well for this," she added. "I promise,"

The exasperated doctor huffed as he climbed up onto the porch of the boarding house.

Ms. Peace wrung her hands and said, "Alright, then. Follow me."

They made their way to the back bedroom on the first floor. The doctor had never been in this room, but knew of it. . He noticed the cleanliness and how well everything was kept and imagined this was where Ms. Peace stayed shortly after Mr. Peace passed away

Ada stirred and moaned when the doctor came in. She cracked an eye and had her gun out and cocked faster than a wasp could wing. She could barely see and she had a fever.

Ms. Peace put a hand on her shoulder and said, "it is okay, I called the doctor."

Ada was worried about more hunters from Mexico that still might be in the town. She had been dreaming about the bandits and whoever it was that sent them. She imagined men busting into the boarding house and filling her body full of bullets as she lay wounded and broken. She saw, in her dreams, everyone in town dead around her surrounded by sandy pools of blood, with flies and vultures the only sources of movement.

"Alright, doc, do what ya have ta," Ada mustered and thanked Ms. Peace.

"Please stop, dear," Ms. Peace said as she held back tears.

Ada owed Ms. Peace an explanation and had to tell her about Therese. She could not clench her fists, so she bit her jaw, and chewed her lip.

As the doctor saw to Ada's many wounds she recounted the story of the shelter and the bodies of Therese's people that they found there. She shared what happened their winter months together as well; however, she did not tell Ms. Peace Therese's story. It was a tale that wasn't hers to tell.

Ada hesitated when she thought about the attack. Ada looked at the floor and her hands shook. Ms. Peace wore worry on her face and her eyes were resigned to death. It was heartbreaking for Ada to have to tell her of Therese.

"There was no way out," Ada said. "We was trapped and cornered. Therese knew it and she played her card."

Ada said a little about the posse and how they came to their end. A strong, fine silence filled the room when she was done. Ada knew what Ms. Peace was waiting for and hated to have to give it to her. Therese had worked for Ms. Peace and had found a place where she fit in and was accepted. Here she worked hard and was appreciated. Ms. Peace had been her family.

The doctor had long finished up with suturing Ada's wounds and was now wrapping her in fresh bandages. "Now, do not bust those sutures. You need plenty of rest and to keep those wounds clean. Lord, I haven't seen anything like that since the war," he said as he wiped his brow.

"We will," Ms. Peace said as she showed him out.

"Thanks doc," Ada spoke up. "Ya both saved me, Ah don't know Ah'm worth it," she added.

"You are," the doctor stated. He tipped his hat to Ada as he departed.

Outside the boarding house, Ms. Peace swore him again to silence. "You cannot say anything, I need to keep this girl safe."

"I know Ms. Peace, I won't speak a word," the doctor said.

That night, after seeing to Ada and hearing her story, the doctor slept in his office. He drank from a bottle of whiskey that his father had left him and had his gun laid on his desk oiled and ready should the need arise. He wrapped himself in silent darkness hoping to go unnoticed.

Ada met Ms. Peace's eyes when she entered the room. Tears brimmed in the widow's eyes as Ada told her of Therese. "Ah buried her well, with prayers and all," Ada swore. "Ah gave her one of those big New Orleans tombs," Ada said as she looked off into the distance.

Ms. Peace's sleep later that night was plagued with nightmares and sadness. "Ms. Picou will have all the time she needs to heal," Ms. Peace swore.

After that day, the indomitable Ms. Peace never had a steady hand again.

Ms. Peace brought food to Ada once per day. During that time, they would sit and talk, though it was Ms. Peace who talked most. Her mind fell back on her memories.

"Small comforts in a harsh world," Ms. Peace would say.

Ada felt guilty about taking up Ms. Peace's time and food. "Ah can't burden you forever," she said. "All Ah got was pesos," she said as she gave them all over to Ms. Peace. "Ah want to pay my way with what Ah got," Ada explained, "Ah owe ya much."

Ms. Peace shoved it away and said, "What you did for Therese was enough." Ms. Peace's eyes held Ada's, and Ada could do nothing but nod.

"Where is William?" Ada asked as her eyes shifted to the door.

"He has been out there in your valley all winter," Ms. Peace said quietly. She looked worried and Ada bit her lip and furrowed her brow.

"Shit," Ada punched the bed and immediately caught herself. "Ah'm sorry mam," Ada stammered.

Ms. Peace looked stern for a moment and then released a laugh., "Fool man, huh?"

"Yeah," Ada looked to the floor. "Fool man."

Word eventually made it through the town that the posse that had shot up Peace's Place were all dead. A few men from town rode and out and verified it days later.

"Looked like the war," observed one.

Another noted, "Whatever happened out there, nobody could'a made it."

The tension in the town broke. Everyone threw fewer looks over their shoulders and stepped lightly as they went about their work. Almost everyone, was comforted by this development. Most townspeople found peace and quiet preferable. Life was fraught with enough challenges and hardships without creating more.

However, Reginald Minger was not one of these people. He was neither happy nor relieved. Decked out his sharp suit and crisp shirt, he did his best to stay composed in Mr. Guilford's office. He was in a heated argument with Mr. Guilford that anyone could hear all the way out to sandy street.

"I need that land, I will have that land," Minger yelled.

Mr. Guilford sat like a statue. He was cool in the face of violence. "No eastern green yokel babe off the teat is going to saunter through my office and raise a ruckus, not without going through the laws of the territory," he stated. "Ms. Picou's land may be adjacent to yours—"

"It's surrounded by my land," Reginald interrupted. His veins popped from his forehead. "She has been missing for months," he continued, "I'm sure her land has gone fallow and her herd—what little she had—has wandered off. Nobody has been out there," he continued.

Mr. Guilford knew Ada had left after the gunfight at Peace's. Neither her body, nor the body of Ms. Peace's help, had been found at the bloody scene. He, as many others had, assumed they had left town and were probably either in Mexico City by now, or dead. "The land is still her land. Squatters can lay claim after so many years pass, but not months." Guilford was concerned with that and had taken precautions. "If Ada does not return, then I would follow the law of the territory." Mr. Guilford was not sure what bothered him about Minger most. Maybe everything about the man was just designed to rile another man up. Minger was an angst-ridden middle-aged man from the east. He dressed too well, spoke down on folks, and acted entitled. When it came right down to it, there just wasn't anything likable about the man.

"She isn't dead and until I see a body, but you can squat all you like. Just remember folks around here might not take a shine to your choices."

Mr. Guilford watched Reginald Minger stalk off and decided to send out a few telegrams.

Time passed and Ada's wounds were starting to heal, but everyone carried their scars differently.

"I'd been a field officer in the war," the doctor said to Sheriff Pile. The two were deep into a bottle of alcohol.

"Yeah, I know you served," replied Johnny.

"I just wanted to head west and retire in a wide-open land where I could be alone. I'd seen too damn much."

"I was in the war too you know," Pile said. He was a rough Confederate looking to retire in a settled town. "Ain't nothing around here as good as this town."

"I didn't come here looking for more war," the doctor slurred.

"Me neither."

Both looked at Peace's Place reflected in the foggy, warped mirror.

"I really wish I'd a caught those fells that shot the place up." Pile slammed his glass down and drew an eye from the bartender.

"That Picou woman beat you to it." The doctor grumbled.

"Did she now," Pile said as he set down the glass of whiskey he was about to down. "She surely didn't make it out of that hell, did she," he asked slyly.

The doctor slurred and sputtered, but it was enough. Johnny Pile knew Ada had killed those Mexicans and, what's more, she was alive. She had stolen the glory from him and now she was hiding in town.

Eager to make his way, Johnny Pile was not subtle. "Where is she," he asked the doctor.

The doctor shook his head, his eyes straying to the mirror.

"Ah, I see," Sheriff Pile said as he pushed out his barstool and stood up. He tipped his hat to the bartender and was gone.

He sought out Ada to ask her where the bandits had come from. Along the way to Peace's, Pile stopped at every shop looking for Ms. Peace. He told everyone where Ada likely was and that she was alive. Before he went into Peace's Place, he stopped by the law office.

"You damned fool," spat Mr. Guilford. "If the woman wasn't dead, she will be now." Mr. Guilford had received replies to his telegrams and he threw them on the desk for the sheriff to see.

Wanted -- Murder -- Railroad Foreman -- Dangerous -- Minger.

The day had been long and hot. The horses stood by the h-brace and sweated as they swatted at a cloud of flies. There was a commotion of food being prepared in the kitchen of a stately ranch house as a warm wind pushed through the heat and wrapped around the building.

Minger sat in the shade of the porch smoking a cigar. He chuckled when he thought of how he had picked this ranch house up at auction. "The look on those yokels' faces," he sneered. "This land is like me: raw, powerful, and untamed," he said to one of his hired guns. "It took some time, but the loan officer foreclosed on the place and moved this family to Michigan. It's a game, really," he observed. "You just need to know how to win."

He could not help but brag. All he needed now was that Picou women's track and he would win no matter the cost.

The man Ada knew as the Preacher drifted through town. Ada, resting and healing at Ms. Peace's, was unaware. People in the street avoided his cold and snake-like eyes.

The Preacher smiled when he caught word of Ada's survival. A cold, hard glint of steel glimmered in his eyes. They were eyes that had witnessed many deaths. Only the man's eyes stood out; he blended in with an average height and an average build. His clothes were basic and functional, but always dark. The hat he wore was worn and stained, as well as a bit frayed at the edges. So long as people didn't see his eyes, he faded into the background and people would have had a hard time placing him.

He looked like a cow punch, that is, until they saw his eyes. His piercing blue gaze could pin a man's very soul to the ground. His eyes were full of a depth of hatred for all mankind. The Preacher had no regard for life and carried out his orders and jobs without passion before he moved on to the next. Clinical and severe, he accepted all proposals that ended in killing and had a particular passion for hunting people.

Many men, organizations, and a few women, had hired him to perform their will. Almost always it was to remove an obstacle or exact retributions. His fortunes had amassed over time; however, there was nothing he wanted. He lived frugally and for the contacts. Over the years he had become numb until nothing excited him except taking a life. The two ways he preferred to kill were with a knife or his bare hands. He looked down on gunslingers.

A thin white smile cracked his face as he recalled his many victims. Eventually he thought on his next.

He rolled a smoke in a shadowy corner outside the stable. The stable boy calmly brushed Ada's roan and was getting tack ready for him. Further confirming what he'd heard, the Preacher was pleased to find that Ada was alive and in riding shape.

Mr. Reginald Minger would not be pleased.

Another smile split the Preacher's face, but it did not reach his eyes. "I'll kill you yet, Picou, but not before I've had my fun, you and yours deserve the worst I got," he said before he crushed the smoldering remains of his cigar under his boot.

Sunshine warmed the wooden boards at Ada's feet. She flexed her toes in the beams and smelled the wood walls while thinking of her home. She stood barefoot in the back door and smelled the breeze. It carried with it the hints of spring and the promise of an end to winter.

Ada knew William was on the ranch, but she still worried about her cattle. He was not as good a shot as she was, she remembered as she thought back to that day with the wolf.

"The calves that made it through the winter needed protection," Ada reflected. She worried about William as well. "Ah need to go," Ada said resolutely as she pulled her socks and boots on.

CHAPTER TWELVE

Minger watched a lone rider amble up to the ranch house; there was no mistaking who it was.

The man known to Ada as the Preacher and Blue Eyes to Reginald Minger hitched his horse to a rail and sat beside him like family. He still wore a smile that refused to go to his eyes.

"What is 'this' about," Minger flicked his gaze to his blue-eyed visitor. "You look like the cat that swallowed the canary."

"I don't much like cats," came the response.

Minger sighed. "Always so damn literal and limited," he said as he chewed his cigar. He leaned in and remarked, "You have no imagination or vision."

"I kill," Blue Eyes said with a shrug. "What could be more visionary or beautiful in this here life? Besides, I'm doing your work, your hands stay clean like that lily white shirt collar you have on."

Minger got a chill while looking into those blue eyes. He shifted a bit in his chair on the porch and looked out across the land. He found Blue Eyes' view of death unsettling. "Hey now, did you find more men?" Minger changed the subject. "We will need a few more hands to button things up around here—"

"Nah, after that last batch you lost none are too willing."

"Drunk fools earned their eternal rest," Minger said with a disdain for anyone south of the Rio Grande.

The air was heavy with heat and stillness as the sun beat down and baked the earth. Minger fanned himself and leaned back in his chair in the shade while looking at anything but the man with the blue eyes.

"Do you want to know why I am here," Blue Eyes asked, breaking the silence.

"You didn't bring me any help, so what is it," an impatient Minger shot back.

"Just thought you would like to know that Miss Ada Picou is alive and well." Blue Eyes paused while letting that information set in. "Plus, she is fit to ride," he added.

Minger's face turned a deep shade of red. He stood and in a single swift motion hurled his chair at the wall. It shattered and busted out a window. A table followed, then another chair. Reginald Minger's fury was not spent until everything around him had been destroyed and the once fine wood furnishings lay broken and shattered all over the porch.

There was no noise from inside the house. Minger cursed and slammed his fists against the walls. Spittle flew as he yelled for his horse. The man with the blue eyes smiled to himself and was glad he had ridden out.

"Ah'm fit and ready as Ah'll ever be," Ada told Ms. Peace. "Ah ain't gonna take any more advantage of your kindness. It's high time Ah rode out."

Ada needed to put eyes on her land. Her guns were cleaned and loaded, ready for whatever she might find.

Ms. Peace stepped forward and blocked Ada from leaving.

"My wounds is healin fine." Ada said. But Ms. Peace stood her ground.

"Surely, you are not fit to ride Ada," Ms. Peace said as she held her arm out and blocked Ada's way.

"Ms. Peace, Ah'm grateful for ya and yer kindness, but Ah gotta a git."

"Ada, I am sure your cattle are fine. William has been watching the place. What is that place to you, that you would go so quick," asked Ms. Peace.

"A home," answered Ada quietly.

It was, she realized, just that. All that time of digging and stacking, the many months with the cattle. . . she felt something for that land. Maybe Jack had seen it in her. She was feeling settled for the first time since she was young, like something had grown in her. Right now Ada wanted nothing more than to get back to the valley and maybe even that dog.

Ms. Peace nodded in understanding, sighed, and stepped aside. "This boarding house is my home," Ms. Peace said quietly in understanding.

"We all gotta have a space," Ada added with a face that was all screwed up and her brow furrowed. "Don't we?"

Ms. Peace held Ada in her arms. "You will always have a place here, Miss Ada Picou, I promise you that." There was a knowing in her eye when she looked at Ada and the two women nodded to one another.

"Ah'll repay the stay and the medicinals—"

"No," came a quiet answer. "There's nothing to repay me for. Just don't get yourself killed," Ms. Peace added.

Ada loaded her saddle and herself onto the quarter horse and rode out from behind the boarding house.

People about doing their business looked up at her passing and gaped. There were a few gasps and a few confused looks. A few folks froze.

Ada threw a sheepish grin at the lot of them and a waved at anyone that made eye contact. Ada turned and noticed that the front of Ms. Peace's boarding house had been partially patched up, but still looked a rough mess.

"Those wounds would never be fully covered," she said under her breath.

The first person she talked to was the boy from the stable. He looked thrilled to see her.

"Hello, Miss," he said as Ada approached.

Ada only realized at that moment how much like Therese he looked. As she crossed the street to collect her roan, a shot rang out.

Ada froze as a blossom of red appeared on the boy's leg.

The boy fell over with a pained and confused look playing across his face. A small cloud of dust arose when he fell forward and landed hard on his face, knocking himself unconscious.

Ada jumped off her horse and checked him. He was out cold. She picked him up and ran with everything that she had back to Peace's Place.

Ms. Peace, summoned by the sound of gunfire no doubt, met her in the door. "Ada, what is happening?" Ms. Peace's voice stopped.

Ada splayed the stable boy out on the table and gave Ms. Peace a fierce look before running back out into the street. There was a commotion behind her as Ms. Peace called out to her, but she did not turn around.

Another shot rang out and Ada rolled behind a trough as the sand by her foot exploded. The shots were coming down from above.

Ada stole a glance and saw people everywhere were running to get off the street.

After a few moments, almost everyone was clear and inside somewhere. Only the blood from the stable boy marred the empty street.

Above and behind where the stable boy had fallen Ada saw an open window. She quickly threw two shots off her hip with one of her pistols. She looked to the quarter horse where her rifle remained still in its scabbard.

Time slowed and seconds stretched out. Beads of sweat stung Ada's eyes and trickled down her back. Muscles taut and ready, she dove and slid her way over to the general store.

Wood exploded behind her as another shot echoed in the street.

Once inside the store, Ada's eyes took a moment to adjust. Mr. Carter was loading his shotgun and a few townspeople were huddling behind the counter.

"Stairs," yelled Ada.

Mr. Carter motioned behind him with his head and had a hard look in his eye. "Stay low, girl," he growled after her.

Ada stuck to the floor and away from the windows. Something on Mr. Carter's counter caught her eye and, a moment later, she was bolting up the stairs behind the counter two at a time

Ada had a plan.

She climbed a ladder leading outside while clenching a small package in her mouth. Once on top of the building, she could see the blood in the street and knew she was on the right rooftop. However, she could not see the window that was open above the stable.

"Whoever the fuck ya are, ya picked the wrong person ta bushwhack," she said under her breath as she sized up her route. The false-faced buildings were close together and Ada leapt from one to another while ignoring the pain in her side. Had she looked, she would've seen her sutures torn and fresh blood staining her clothes.

Wood flew from the roof on her right as another rapport issued from the hidden rifleman.

"Ya missed, ya piss drink'n yella bestard," Ada yelled. She landed on the stable roof and her boots slid. A shot passed by her leg and blasted through the roof. "Sonofabitch, ya gittin closer, ya blind ass," Ada yelled again continuing her onslaught taunts.

She heard cursing beneath her and the sound of someone hastily reloading a rifle.

Ada looked across the roofline and through the hole made by the bullet in the rooftop under her. She shifted her position and rolled away as two more rounds hit the rooftop. Her ears rang and her eyes stung as Ada thrust herself off the roof grunting.

As she flew through the air she turned and let fly a lit stick of dynamite that arced into the black maw of the open window.

There was a moment of silence as she fell through the air. Time seemed to turn to molasses. A moment later, a tremendous roar erupted from the second floor of the stable and she was blasted from the air to the ground below.

The entire contents of the second story were vomited into the street. Bedding, glass, metal, and indistinguishable chunks of what was

once a living being were hurled to the dirt road below and smoke
billowed from the building's remains.

Chapter Thirteen

Ada could barely make out the sounds of people screaming over the ringing in her ears. She was in excruciating pain and her sense of balance was completely thrown off. The street filled with debris, smoke, and townspeople. Nothing was clear and she could barely press herself from the ground.

Ada's blurred vision cleared first. Her head lolled to one side as she looked around at the people running around in a panic. She tensed and clutched her side, feeling the blood. An unarmed man and woman lifted her out of the flotsam and laid her out on the porch of the saloon nearest the stable.

She did not hear any more shots from the stable. Ada looked wearily at the town.

Someone handed her a flask and said, "Drink this."

It was the sheriff.

"Oh damn, ya arrest'n me," Ada murmured in a slurred voice.

"No, not yet," the sheriff said with his eyes on the stable.

Ada's senses snapped to attention with the homemade brew. "Lordy, sheriff, is this kerosene?" Ada said before she was sick all over the planks.

When she was done, she wiped at her mouth with her arm and looked to the street. "Anyone shot?"

"Everyone alright beside the fella you blew up," someone stated from the growing crowd.

Ada turned toward the damage she caused and asked, "What'a Ms. Peace and Therese's little brother, tha stable boy?" Ada was trying to get up but the world started spinning around her and she fell back to her seat.

The sheriff threw her a sharp look. "We'll get to that corn in a bit. You just sit tight and I'll see about all of this," he said as he got up and started walking toward the stable. "I'll get back to you in a bit."

Sheriff Pile saw all the horses had been let out and spooked by the blast and were roaming the outskirts of the town. "God damn lucky horses." He shook his head and titled his hat back while taking in the damage.

Ada gritted her teeth and braced herself as best she could as she staggered over to the boarding house. Boots heavy like lead, she staggered through the door and saw Ms. Peace and the doctor.

"He saw you carry Abel in," Ms. Peace said indicating the doctor.

"Abel, that's a good name," Ada said as she slid down the wall and her mind darkened into blackness.

Ada dreamed of Therese standing in the snow while backlit by the moon and was holding purple wildflowers in her hand.

Out the corner of her eye, Ada saw Arden running through the woods. One night, the two women had been watching the coals die down and in that time Ada brought up her family to Therese.

"What words do ya have fer the dead," Ada asked.

"We have many," replied Therese. She furrowed her brow and looked at the ground. "Maybe too many," she said softly.

That night, Ada learned a prayer in Spanish from Therese. She did not understand the prayer, but she felt good when saying it.

When Ada came to, she said the prayer for Abel, Arden, Joel, Mary, and Therese.

The sun moved in a fatigued manner across the sky before it set slowly in the west. A calm and quiet night descended on the town. The gentle breeze and animal noises provided a blanket of apparent normality after the hectic day.

In the morning, the smoke from the burning stable was gone, along with most of the stable itself.

The doctor, again, patched Ada up. "I'm begging you Miss Picou, get more rest this time," He said as he cast her sly smile. "And try to not to blow anything else up."

"Ah ain't promise'n nuthin," Ada said as she managed a weak shrug. Stiff and exhausted, she murmured, "Thanks doc, again." She patted his backside before she made her way outside.

"Well, you sure did a number on that fella," Ms. Peace said. She was sitting with Abel on the planks of the walkway and nodded toward the stables.

"Yeah, well, he had it come'n." Ada looked at Abel and his now singular leg. She ruffled his hair and he pulled away from her, both smiling and wincing at the same time.

"You know I've got him, don't you," asked Ms. Peace.

Ada gave her a knowing half-smile. "Yer his family, 'course ya got 'im."

Abel said something in Spanish and Ms. Peace chuckled.

"What's he on about?" Ada asked with a nod at the boy.

"He hopes you visit. Says he likes your horse." Ms. Peace smirked.

Ada smiled to Abel and nodded. "Ah'll be 'round, you tell 'im that." Ada turned and started walking away before they saw the sadness in her eyes.

Once outside and in the morning glare, Ada saw that the damage was worse than she thought. She flagged down Sheriff Pile and shielded her eyes as she asked him, "Who was it?"

"Reginald Minger," Johnny replied.

"Well, Ah'll be damned," Ada whistled gently. "Ah didn't expect that green townie ta go after anyone 'round here. Seemed just a bag o' hot air last time we crossed," Ada said as she thought back to her run in at Mr. Carter's.

"Mr. Guilford tells it he came west looking for fame and fortune. Was looking to lock up and buy this land around here. Tipped off, he was, something about a rail line."

Ada nodded, having seen his type before. Ada cursed. "He stirred up a hornet's nest and found hisself blown up. Bastard should'na come out here and messed with us."

He gave Ada a knowing nod. "He was hunting your land in particular."

Ada stood with her feet flat and shoulders square. "Ah guess he was, jist towing the mark here though. Anyone worth their salt woulda' done the same, Ah jist beat 'em to it." Their eyes fell upon the remains of the stable's mangled roof.

Johnny offered Ada his hand and Ada shook it.

"Sorry Ah beat you to it Sheriff Pile."

"Ada, the people don't want you in town no more, and I can't say that I blame them." He looked at what was left of the stable.

She looked over the town and thought for a moment. "Yeah, Ah don't either," she said as she walked off toward the horses outside of town and adjusted her hat.

Ada felt the tug in her belly drawing her to home as the valley she had settled in was pulling at her to return. As she was walking away from Sheriff Johnny Pile, Mr. Guilford stopped her.

"Bad business, that one," Mr. Guilford said while indicating to the stables. "I received a telegraph about Reginald Minger and was about to put Johnny on him. Turns out he was a wanted man back east. Word was he murdered a few folks."

Ada sighed. "It weren't tha Preacher," she said as she gazed up to the sky.

"No Ada, it *weren't*. But he definitely wanted you dead and he did hire that man for his crew."

"Yeah well, guess Ah ain't that easy to put down," she replied.

"Johnny tell you about what he was after?"

"Yep," Ada said.

"Lately, he'd been scooping up tracts around Jack Flynn's place. Mr. Reginald Minger used to work for a railway and learned where a proposed track was heading. He planned to put a depot and then some businesses."

"Clever bastard," Ada spat.

Both silently nodded.

"Mr. Flynn wouldn't sell, Reginald Minger harassed him and made his life miserable, I only recently learned of it," Mr. Guilford continued. "I am truly sorry Miss Picou, if I would have known—"

Ada flashed a grin and punched him the in the arm.

Mr. Guilford let out a choked laugh before he quickly regained his composure. "He got desperate when he sent those bandits after you."

"Hot damn, so he really hired 'em," Ada said. "This entire time Therese and Ah wasn't sure what they were about, bastard," she spat. "He got her killed. Ah sure as hell wouldn't've been so damn careful." She stood straight and wiped at her face.

Mr. Guilford looked from Ada to the stable and muttered, "*careful*," before shaking his head.

Sheriff Pile walked over from the Sheriff's Office. "You want me to ride out with you Ms. Ada," he asked.

"Nah, thanks Johnny," Ada said as she thumbed her belt. "Ah'll ride on alight, thanks though." Ada tipped her hat and walked up to the roan. She struggled to get on, but made it without reopening her wounds.

He chuffed and stamped, tail alight. The dark red quarter horse followed.

"Both ya'll need a good brush'n and Ah know yer hooves are a sight," Ada said as she adjusted herself in the saddle and set out. She wondered what she would find at their place. "Did that yella bastard tear it down," she asked the roan.

His ears twitched.

"Did he run off, or kill the cattle," she wondered. As she rode, she thought about the dog and all of the death that seemed to go wherever she did. It chased her like a shadow, her eternal companion.

Chapter Fourteen

"If its destroyed, we'll rebuild. If the cattle died, we'll breed more." Ada said to herself as she rode. She knew how to endure even when all was stacked against her. "Ain't gonna get no help though." She sighed back at the town that receded into the distance behind her.

Ada reflected on the life of Therese as she rode. "A woman hunted to her end," Ada sighed.

It was a small comfort to know that she had helped kill Alejandro and his men. Ada missed the small Mexican woman. Therese's was a calming presence to Ada, especially those prayers she would say low under her breath. When Therese had said them, there was a quiet power to them that settled Ada's nerves.

Eventually Ada was met with the view of green grass pushing through the remaining slush from winter.

"Don't look as bad Ah thought," she said to the horses. She went up to the animal stalls and found that they were charred and empty. However, she was shocked that the cattle looked healthy and the numbers looked right. She counted once and then a second time to confirm.

As she rode up to her shelter, a man stepped out.

"Welcome home," William greeted her with a grin. He was standing in the doorway with a shotgun.

Ada noticed the walls around him were pockmarked with bullet holes and was speechless.

Coming through between William's knees and into the light of day was the dog. It wagged its tail upon seeing Ada.

Taking it all in, Ada swung down to the ground. She felt her heavy spirit lifting.

William set down the gun and trod over to her. Without saying a word, they embraced each other. Time meant nothing to them.

"Ah thought ya were dead," Ada said into his chest.

"I thought the same of you," William breathed in the smell of her hair. "You don't know how glad I am you made it back," he added.

But she knew. Ada felt it in his heartbeat.

Spring unfolded with a measured grace. Ada and William occupied themselves with putting everything back together. Plants spurted up through the softening ground and flowers unfurled, drawing all manner of insects to their sweet nectar. The south wind shifted and brought with it both warmth and chirruping birds.

Ada and William found peace in their day-to-day lives while working the ranch. During this time, Ada bought a flatbed wagon and was able to bring in more wood. William split his time between the general store and the place he was building with Ada. He saw how much she loved the land and they both put their efforts into making improvements.

Ada reworked the irrigation While William fell trees north of the salt veins. Together they planed the wood. Soon, a new stable was built. Now they had was a washbasin and better bedding in the home. Ada even retooled the doors that had been shot to pieces.

He and Ada were sitting by their hearth together and enjoying the warmth of the fire when William began telling the tale of what happened after Ada disappeared.

"When you escaped from town," William explained, "those Mexicans came here. They must have thought you'd head here. I thought so too," he stated. "As soon as I realized you weren't in town, I saddled up and rode here with the bandits close behind. They rode off the cattle and killed a few head. They saw my horse and thought it was you, so I ducked in here. I'm glad this place was built of stone," he reminisced on that frightful time with a smile.

"Not sure how many shots they fired, but they shot it to hell," William continued talking and Ada listened intently. "I only had my shotgun and not much for it. When they couldn't get into the house— seeing as I shot anyone who tried—they burnt the stable down. My horse had run off."

Ada nodded. She could clearly see everything in her mind.

"I was sure I was dead," William sighed. "There were so many casings that it looked like a war was fought here."

"Why ain't ya dead then." Ada, head cocked, interrupted with a little humor in her voice.

"It's thanks to your friends the tribal folk living nearby. They were crossing your land up the valley and must'a seen the ruckus."

"They was coming back from a big hunt; they were all armed to the teeth and in a fury." William spoke with awe in his voice and looked up toward the sky. "Like a storm opened up, they rode down on those fellas," he described the scene. "There were war cries and firing, and horses were everywhere. Everything around here got torn up. The bandits were caught off guard and didn't stand a chance," he said with gratitude in his voice.   "When they were run off, some of the native people came to the house. I left the shotgun inside when I heard one call your name."

"I put my hands up and stepped outside," he continued. "I told them what happened at Peace's and they didn't say anything, just listened. One came back after a bit with my horse. Told me you would be back; I knew he was right. I spent a few weeks in the cold piling up shells and arrows. Collected a whole lot of 'em. I burned the bodies that were left behind because I was worried about diseases, and especially of the wolves getting their scent. Those natives didn't come back here, but I saw lone scouts on the ridge looking out. They kept an eye on this house as much as I did."

Ada nodded, promising to herself to thank the natives when she next got the chance.

"When the snow melted, I rode herd and rounded up what I could. Your brand stands out clear," he stated.

"Yeah," Ada took the compliment in stride. "That was Jack's idea. Told me ta keep it clear and simple." she said. A moment later, she eyed William up and stated, "Ah owe ya."

"Nah," William said quickly. "You're good people."

"Ya are too, Billy."

Before now, Ada had only called him William.

William's face reddened as he stood and gathered some fresh wood for the fire.

Ada thought about the time that she spent here on her land and the people of the nearby town. This part of her life gave her some hope. Even so, the loss of Therese still weighed upon her heart.

In the morning Ada counted the herd. A few were gone, but less than she'd feared before her return. What remained were strong and stout.

Ada hunted on the roan; the quarter was skittish, but was warming up to her. As spring slowly unfolded, Ada and William replenished their supplies. It was a marker for normalcy when Ada felled her first deer. William and Ada worked together to dress the kill and prepare the meat. Truly this was the life.

William had never been around anyone like Ada Picou. Brought out west young, he had watched his parents die of yellow fever. Mr. Guilford, the Peaces, and Mr. Carter took care of him after that. He belonged to the town as much as it did to him. People thought for a while he would become sheriff, but Johnny Pile was more hungry for it. William was not a peacekeeper in that way. He was just candid and had a way of settling folks down. During disputes, Mr. Guilford would look to William to talk people. He had a calming way about him and was always clear about his reasoning, earning the respect of all that dealt with him.

When she was ready, Ada told William about Reginald Minger and the boy from the stable.

"I know them both well," William said. "Ms. Peace has been there for them since they came to town." He shifted uneasily. "I hope that boy is alright. He was damn good in that stable."

Ada eventually also told William about the winter she shared with Therese. They passed a flask of whiskey and watched the stars as she recounted her tale. "Ah hope with all my heart Therese and her folks found peace," Ada said. She drank deeply as she recalled the sermons of Therese's people.

Once Ada went quiet, William spoke up while looking into the sky, "Maybe we end up stars."

"Yea," Ada replied, "can hope fer it."

The flatbed wagon made life easier and helped move things along at a brisk pace. Ada could carry more stones now, and she did so with vigor. It was also easier to retrieve salt in better quantities, so the stores at the house improved. Two stalls were added where one had stood, and tack room was also put up in an addition. William also continued his work on the small building where they'd do their curing.

Every day was filled with activity. One day, Ada showed William how she used a rifle and tested his skills against hers.

"Yer a natural." Ada smiled. "Yer aim's true."

"Only with the rifle," he answered humbly.

"Yeah, ya stick to the rifle, Ah'll handle the pistols."

A couple days later, Ada asked out of the blue, "So, when'r ya fetch'n yer things?"

The next day William rode the flatbed wagon into town to collect his belongings. He was excited and in a hurry, but made himself take his time.

Ms. Peace looked at him with a bittersweet smile. "I'm happy for you William, but you better visit."

Mr. Guilford called to William when he passed and said, "I see you're homesteading now."

"Yes sir," a smile broke out across William's placid face.

"Well son, this town has always watched out for you and will continue to." He paused and weighed his words, a pause that William noticed. "As a matter of fact, well, son, I'm getting long in the tooth." Mr. Guilford sighed as he looked out over the town. "I'm tired," he said. "We—the town—have decided to make you our next lawyer. You will represent us." William raised his hands and was about to protest, but Mr. Guilford stopped him.

"Now, now, don't worry, everything will go well."

"How could I be a lawyer," William stuttered in shock. "You are our town's lawyer. . . I just don't understand what you are saying Mr. Guilford."

"Well, son, after you study my law books, you head into El Paso and take a test. I will help you prepare."

William stood on the sand of main street and was utterly speechless.

"Now you head out and we will see about things after you and that Ada Picou get yourselves settled. It's a good spot." He squinted at the sun. "Maybe the best around." He nodded to William. "Enjoy the rest of your day, son." Mr. Guilford turned and walked off without another word, leaving a weighty silence behind him.

"Mr. Guilford, wait a second! What about the stable, what happened," William asked upon noticing the remains of the stable and the portions that'd already been rebuilt.

Mr. Guilford glanced at the repairs being made. He sat on a bench outside his office And William joined him.

Mr. Guilford recounted the events leading up to Minger's explosive death.

William reflected on what Ada left out. She was humble and not prone to brag, after all. Upon Mr. Minger finishing his tale, William stood and said, "Thank you Mr. Guilford." His eyes swept the town and took everything in.

William and Mr. Guilford shook hands.

"You all have been there for me," William stated, "and I will be there for you."

"I know my boy, I know."

It took William a few days to make it back to the valley where Ada was waiting. As he came into the valley, he saw a strange horse by the new stalls. A feeling of panic came over him and his heart raced as he worried that something may have happened to Ada.

Riding down as swift as the wind, it wasn't until he was close that he saw it was a native's pony.   The noise of the fast-moving wagon—now fully loaded—drew out Ada and her guest.

William had seen this man once before. This man had been the one who returned his horse. They nodded to each other and the visitor leaped onto his pinto before striking off north.

Ada was quiet and tense. William could see her biting her jaw and guessed that her mind was somewhere far away. She had a fierce look in her eyes.

"Why tha hell didn't ya tell me," she said coldly.

William sat in silent ignorance and was unsure of what he had failed to say.

"The Preacher," she spoke indignantly, "he rode through here."

William sat down in the wagon and, after a bit of thought, remembered a man who had come by in the winter. He had been alone and on guard.

"A cow punch had come through," said William. "He didn't say much. It was snowing, about the night after that big storm broke." William explained, "I let him take shelter with me." "Ada, was he. . .?"

Ada was silent. William dreaded this silence. He could feel the invisible weight hanging over Ada.

"He's tha man that killed my family," Ada said. Her eyes were distant and cold, her jaw tight.

For the second time in one day, William was stunned into silence. "Ada, I didn't know," he eventually said once he regained his wits. His heart raced in his chest. William jumped down from the wagon and went over to her. He had expected to tell her about Mr. Guilford's proposal, but this conversation was more pressing. He was looking forward to showing her the new rifle he had bought, but didn't get the chance.

All William and Ada envisioned of their future fell away as Ada packed her saddle bags. There was nothing to do but assist her.

"I'm won't try and stop you," William aid while moving around Ada and helping her pack.

"Ya wouldn't dare," Ada said with an icy tone.

William put his hands up. "That's not what I meant. What I mean is I'll come with you."

There was obvious desperation in his voice.

Ada shook her head. "Nah, this is yers as much as mine. Yer blood's in it too." Her eyes took in the tranquil beauty of the range. She jerked her head toward the south. "That town there, that's yers too."

William ran his fingers through his hair and shook the dust from his hat. "Ada, I know what it feels like to be torn. You have my heart as much as the town."

They walked together the new outbuilding and packed some jerk for the rod. William grabbed several cases of shells and handed them to Ada.

The straps covering the bags of supplies were tightened and thrown atop the roan's rump. He was saddled up and chewed at his bit, ready to depart.

Ada stepped back and silently surveyed the horse. Then she looked around and took in all they had done together. Her eyes were wet. "Ah ain't ready, Ah don't deserve it yet," she said, partly to William and partly to herself.

William stood before her, unsure of what else he could do for her.

Ada pulled him into a rib-cracking hug and her breath caught. A moment of silence passed between them. Ada looked up and William, and William down at Ada.

They shared a long kiss. In the brief moment they held onto one another the world fell away.

Eventually Ada pushed away. In one fluid motion, she hooked her boot in a stirrup and lifted herself up into the saddle.

"Yer a good one, Billy, a really good one." Ada said. She looked around the valley and felt nothing but grateful for the land and for him.

William had shed his blood and sweat right along with her on this land and her heart was heavy at the thought of leaving it all behind. Still, she could not enjoy it until she'd seen her first mission to its end.

"Ya deserve this place more'n me right now."

William held her horse's reins, his heart racing. "I'll be here," he responded. His eyes locked on hers. "I'll keep it ready for when you get back," he said with sincerity.

Ada nodded. "Ah know ya will do right by it. Ya love it like Ah do," Ada's voice said in a thick and husky voice.

William released the reins and Ada clicked her tongue. The roan stepped forward, walking north.

Ada rode alone, and the hunt resumed.

As Ada crested the ridge, she turned back and took one last look at the valley. Her home was there, along with Billy who was caring for it. She could see him still standing there where she'd left him by the wagon. A wagon filled with his life.

"Ah'll give it a chance, if Ah make it," Ada promised.

With those final words were whispered to the sky, Ada turned and rode off with the wind at her back.

ACKNOWLEDGMENTS

This book would not exist if not for the support of my family and friends. Thank you Shannon, Gabriele, and Sasha for always believing in me and sticking with me through all of our crazy adventures. Thank you Leyla, Mina, Xander, and Henry for being amazing human beings. Thanks to my parents and my sister Patricia, Nicky, and Kelly. Thank you Craig for your enthusiasm. It also crucial that I recognize the contributions of my editor Jamie Johns, who worked magic with my submissions. She has tolled tirelessly and with great skill to bring this book to life. Thank you Lorna Reid for your amazing formatting artistry. Thank you Mina Perkins for the phenomenal cover art. I would like to take this opportunity to thank Ms. Billy Joe Vary, who was my seventh grade English teacher in Kentucky. She pushed me in class and her belief in me carried me far through this journey. Thank you Mr. Byrd and Mrs. Martin from my high school in Louisiana who suffered through so much of my high school shenanigans, yet never gave up on me. Thank you Alex McKenna whose voice inspired me to write Ada's story. A huge thank you to the amazing people of Acadian Louisiana whose rich history and culture informed so much of my writing.

ABOUT THE AUTHOR

A. B. Parr lives in southeast Louisiana surrounded by family and friends. He enjoys all facets of the western genre and is always looking for ways to expand upon the mythos of the American frontier. His hobbies include reading, biking, hiking, and listening to music. The author holds degrees in History, Special Education, and Behavioral Psychology.

www.abparr.com